home

Nicole Harman

Home. Such an odd word. It's supposed to have meaning and comfort. A place to go to rest. A place to restore oneself at the end of each day. A place to be yourself without explanation.

In the last year, I have lived in three separate areas. Three separate communities. Three separate places people have called my home.

First was Athra. The place I grew up. The place I outgrew.

Then, there was Banshui. The place I was beginning to feel like was home. The place I walked away from.

Now, Encampment for Exes. The place I was taken to. The place Byrein considers to be my home.

I don't.

But to keep myself on good terms with him, I make sure that I am the only one who knows that secret. As far as Byrein is concerned, he has convinced me that this is the place I belong. And he can't seem to see past his victory of my being by his side, and his ever-growing greed for power, to question it. This is something I find myself to be thankful for.

I sat on the strewn-out, rust-colored rug, at the foot of the wood-framed bed in my large canvas-sided tent. I peered at the faded design below me, trying to understand what it once was, before the years robbed it of its beauty. With a soft hand, I lifted the tan bedsheet, exposing the small nicks in the wood I had carved with a small, sharp rock. One for each day I was conscious here. A tally for my own sanity.

"First day of fall. The leaves always rustle a bit different on the first day," someone noted. I listened to two people's footsteps as they passed by my tent.

First day of fall. Happy birthday, Esmari. Happy

belated birthday to you too, Hunter. One day late. Sorry, Hunter, my best friend. I sighed and looked over my notches once again. I was certainly missing several from the days I had spent here, unconscious. Taking the small smooth tan rock into the pads of my fingers, I carved the additional tallies that were missing, listening to the satisfying scrape the wood made.

This would be the second birthday without my childhood best friend. Last year it stung. This year, however, it hurt in an entirely different way.

This birthday marked something significant. I was of marrying age. At least the age I set for myself. As soon as one has their wings, they are of marrying age, to society, that is. But for me, I personally had said I would wait at least two birthdays to consider the thought of finding someone. Not a moment sooner.

Now, that seemed such a silly concept. A concept created and dreamed up by such a whimsical and starry-eyed girl once upon a time. A concept that was delusional and illogical.

I tossed the rock back by the foot of the bed and slid the stiff sheet back down to cover my carvings. *I wonder if Byrein knows it's your birthday, Es.* I shuddered at the thought. I couldn't imagine how he might treat me differently.

Byrein has treated me like a prize he won since we arrived. And he made sure that everyone else knew where I stood in the hierarchy: well above them. I learned immediately where I stood as well. It was simple. I had to know to survive. But I also quickly learned how to use it to my advantage. With the people in the community here, and with Byrein himself.

While I was below Byrein in this Encampment hierarchy, I found that each day I was gaining more of his trust. I knew how to talk to him and around him. With each new day here, it became more second nature. I knew how to hold myself steady and sure in his presence, keeping an even, unwavering tone. I had learned what words to use, and which words were triggers. I played the part he wanted, but I was taking control of it all, little by little.

Slowly, but surely, I was manipulating this game of his, and I was manipulating him. I knew when to test the boundaries and when to step back. I had learned how to guide conversations in ways that I wanted them to go. Byrein's obsession over me as his prize clouded his judgment at times. I have found just how to utilize my tone in my voice and some of the trigger words or topics with him to gain control of situations.

I had to be careful, though.

If I was too confident, or showed that I was doing any of this on purpose, Byrein might catch on. He might realize that he is being manipulated and not in complete control of the situation. For me, that could be very bad.

I stood with a sigh and dusted myself off. Scrunching at my toes, I adjusted my slippers on my feet, happy that they were a barrier between my skin and the cool hard ground below.

For a moment I listened. I savored the silence and peace of privacy. Something I had come to crave. It was rare that I had time to myself. And it was something I just recently earned from Byrein. I had spent weeks gaining his trust, little by little, convincing him that I would stay, and convincing him that I deserved some privacy.

At first Byrein tried to remain by my side at all times. I absolutely hated it. He wanted to be the one who saw I had gone to sleep in my designated tent at night; and that I had gotten up in the morning the same way.

I detested it from the very first day. I would note that I wanted to make myself presentable for him. I played it up as if I were higher maintenance than I really am. I tried to convince him that this would be inappropriate, being that I was a lady, and he was man, and the others were sure to talk about it. I didn't want there to be any gossip. I assured him that he didn't want the gossip either. His followers may just look down on me.

He took the bait.

But unfortunately, he gave me an "assigned help." He claimed that she was there to help me with my daily tasks. The menial things, like washing my clothing, or fluffing my sheets, making sure my needs are met, all were to be taken care of by her. He claimed it was so that I could focus my energy on more important matters. I knew that she was just there to keep an eye on me and make sure I didn't run off.

Millie, my assigned help, was originally supposed to be at my side any moment that I wasn't by Byrein's. Just recently, I somehow managed to convince Byrein to give me some personal space first thing in the morning.

I remember noting that I missed having time to focus myself and my power first thing in the morning without another person's power distracting me. Honestly, I think it was a borderline, backhanded remark, but the following day, I woke up to a peaceful morning without Millie sitting at her chair by the foot of my bed. I didn't dare question it.

I closed my eyes and listened for the sound of the outside world. The one I knew very well I would need to venture out into, soon enough. The one filled with all sorts of people I barely knew anymore. The place I had to put on a show at all times, for my own safety.

I wanted to pause time. I wanted to hide forever. Because here in the peace and quiet of my tent, at least I could have just one more moment where I didn't need to be aware of my posture or facial expressions. I didn't need to respond to anyone. Not here. Not now. Not right in this moment of the morning.

With a slow, steady release of air, I breathed. I smelled the earthiness around me. The smell of the fall trees just outside graced my nostrils. If it were different circumstances, I might actually like this place. It had beauty.

"Miss Esmari?" called a voice. Millie's powerful presence was evident just outside the flaps of my tent opening.

I drew my even-toned voice out of my throat. "Yes?"

"Byrein requests your presence this morning," her voice called through.

Right. "I will be out shortly," I responded. Turning toward my vanity.

"Miss Esmari?"

"Yes, what is it?" I answered.

"Byrein has asked for you to wear the blue today," she relayed.

Of course he does.

"One more thing, Miss Esmari," Millie breathed.

"What is it?" I remarked with a twinge of sass.

"Byrein has asked if you have any request of what to have for your breakfast, Miss," she stated, disregarding my tone.

He's asking what I want? How unusual. "I am not too hungry this morning. But, I would love a nice warm tea."

Just the thought of having a warm tea seeping

down my dry throat made the morning seem less dreary. And it's not often that I get to request what I would like to have.

"Thought you might, Miss Esmari. I will let him know." If I wasn't mistaken, I could have sworn that Millie smiled as she responded to me.

I turned and stepped to the wardrobe sitting at the side of my vanity. With a tug, I pulled at the small golden handles and opened its doors, revealing the minimal amount of clothing I was provided, all of which, besides my sleepwear, were dresses or gowns. It seemed too fancy to wear this kind of stuff all the time, but Byrein said it made me look more important than the rest of the people. Honestly, I just wished that I could wear pants and a tee shirt again.

Of course, Byrein requested the blue dress. I sighed, crinkling my nose up at it. I hated the blue one. It had itchy lace on the sleeves and the fabric was stiff. I thought it was atrocious.

I pondered for a moment. I had several other dresses I could wear. All of which would be more comfortable that that awful blue one. I could just smear it in the dirt and say that it was not presentable. But then, he might find Millie to blame, and knowing how long his night was the night before, who knows how he would lash out at her. Knowing him, I would have a new assigned help, and likely never see her again.

I shook my head. It would be a shame, I like Millie. She was nice enough. More importantly, she didn't bother me much.

Pulling the dress from the wardrobe, I looked it over. *You really should have destroyed this dress a long time ago, Es.* I tried not to groan at it.

Carefully, I changed into the requested attire. I braided my hair back, out of my face. Dusting off my feet on the mostly clean rug beside my bed, I slipped into my shoes. I took the opportunity to pause once more at full mirror perched to the side of my tent opening, making sure I would meet Byrein's standards.

My fingertips floated to my necklace, toying with the charms hanging from it. I looked over the black onyx and green jade, feeling for the small divot in the back of the round jade. I lost consciousness in a recent Sight episode, and when I woke up I was face down on the ground. The jade stone hasn't been the same since. The black onyx, however, remained the same.

You shouldn't keep Byrein waiting any longer. With a lift of my hand, I straightened my shoulders and pulled the heavy fabric back to exit my tent.

The morning light seeped through the trees of the woods around us. Leaves fell from the branches and dusted the pathway before me. An Ex caught my attention as I walked. Quickly, he paused, swiftly stepping out of the path and bowing his head, allowing me to pass.

"Good morning, Miss Esmari."

I nodded to them.

Another person I came upon greeted me the same.

"Good morning, Miss Esmari," they said, bowing their head as they allowed me to pass.

It was as Byrein had instructed. And he made it abundantly clear that if he were to catch anyone not treating me with the upmost respect, that they would have to deal directly with him. From what I gather, everyone knows not to be on Byrein's bad side.

It all felt too posh. Too formal. The attire I always wore, the nodding at them, rather than greeting, all of it. But, I knew when to pick my battles with Byrein. And this was not one of them.

Plus, this way, more of them steered clear of me, which I personally didn't mind.

I watched as a pumpkin-colored leaf floated down from the nearby tree branch hanging over my pathway, catching a ray of light as it gracefully glided to the earth. Part of me wished I could be like that very leaf. Barely noticed. Only merely existing long enough to be tossed in the morning breeze and forgotten.

I could feel Byrein as I inched closer to his tent. His power was so eminent and strong to me. It terrified me just how in tune I was to its feeling. I suppose that's what happens when you spend every day around it.

I caught his eyes peering back at me from just outside of his tent. He was watching. Though, it didn't surprise me. But his calm demeanor did. He seemed relaxed and ready for the day. Ready to see me. Seemed unusual. Which meant that I needed to be extra careful around him this morning. He could change moods at a moment's notice.

"Hello, my Esmari," Byrein greeted.

"Hello." I kept my voice even and cold, just as I usually did around him.

"How did you sleep last night? Did the wind

keep you up?" Byrein prodded.

I knew he just wanted to get me talking. "I slept well."

Byrein nodded. I could see now in his eyes that he was anxious. His muscles twitched. His black crow-like wings tensed, making the tips of the feathers perk up, before returning to the relaxed state. He took in more power, I could tell, and his body was reacting to the overload. I was right. His mood could change in a matter of moments. He was on edge. I needed to fix that for him, and ultimately, also for me.

"Why don't you tell me about your night over breakfast?" I offered.

"Thank you, my Esmari. You are such a wonderful listener when I need," Byrein breathed with a nod. He placed a hand hovering just over top of my wings resting at my spine. With his other, he waved inside to his little two-person table.

This hand that hovered above me was not out of kindness, or chivalry. He was not trying to be a gentleman by guiding me in. Nor was he being cautious and protective.

He was feeling for my presence of power. Feeling how strong it was. I rarely released any before our breakfast meeting each morning, just in case. The same way I was reading him, he was trying to do the same with me. Though, I was pretty sure that I was a lot better at it than he was.

I took my usual seat and found a steaming hot tea in an ornately painted teacup. One I hadn't seen before. Its brim was lined with a gold paint to match the delicate flowers and vines climbing from the base. I took the spoon from the saucer and scooped a small mound of sugar onto it. Carefully, I watched the grains of sugar fall into the hot liquid, before stirring.

Byrein took his seat and began talking about his experiment. I could feel the tension lessen in his shoulders as he explained each moment in his story. To my understanding, it didn't go as planned, which explains his tension. He doesn't like when things don't work out the way he thinks they will. He ended up taking in someone else's power, but it didn't sound like that was planned either. The person turned on him mid-experiment and he had to make a choice. Or so he says.

"I had to take it from him. His loyalty was faltering. I gave him so much here and then he had the audacity to tell me what he would and wouldn't do with the very power I expanded for him." Byrein pinched at the bridge of his nose. It made me think of Mr. Sean.

"Sir—" someone asked, poking their head into the opening.

"Ah, yes," Byrein said standing. "I'll just be a moment, my Esmari."

Byrein slipped outside and I could hear him conversing with the man. I lifted the tea to my lips. The flavor helped me remember Jewel. I clung to the memories in hope that someday I would see her once again.

I allowed my mind to linger on her memory. I thought of the letters with detailed instructions I had left for my dear sweet friend. I had hoped that she understood. That she was able to follow the instructions. That there were no problems between her or Kasius, or between her and Mr. Sean. It had been months, and I am sure she was frustrated with me. Maybe she was finding comfort in an early morning tea over at the Dripping Crown this morning too. Maybe Victor was providing her a comforting conversation. Maybe she was smiling and rambling on to him about some sort of nonsense.

I closed my eyes and took another sip, pretending that I was with her, back in Banshui, instead of here in the Encampment with Byrein. I imagined her voice in my ears and the way her eyes would light up when she got a sly idea. The way she would bobble her head to music and how Victor and I would laugh.

"My Queen. When you have finished your breakfast tea, it will be time to start our day. You will be joining me today," Byrein instructed, breaking me from my daydream.

A chill ran down my spine. I couldn't tell if it were from the temperature, or from the anxiety riddling my veins. I straightened my shoulders and consciously tried to relax the muscles in my shoulders before Byrein noticed the tension. I swirled the last drops of the liquid in my teacup. I knew I couldn't stretch my time sitting here much longer. Byrein would know what I was trying to stall.

An impatient sigh left his lips. I knew he intended to hurry me. After sipping the last of my tea, I set it gently on its saucer and patted at the corners of my mouth with a napkin. I folded the napkin in half and placed it gently next to the saucer.

Stiffly, I stood and fixed my dress.

I could feel Byrein's eyes on me as I adjusted. I tried my best not to acknowledge his dark gaze. It was prideful. I could feel it. Bothered by my lack of haste no doubt, but prideful in the prize in front of him: me. Not of my accomplishments, or of my power, but of his possession of me. It was disgusting.

"You are ready now," Byrein stated. It wasn't a question. It rarely was.

Byrein strode just ahead of me and pulled the cloth back from the opening of the tent. He glanced back at me with distracted eyes. Likely thinking of all the *knowledge* he will show me today. I wanted to roll my eyes. I stifled a shudder through my bones as I remembered some of the recent lessons he so graciously bestowed upon me.

Maybe I'll stay conscious this time.

He was intense in his teachings. Much like his father, Mr. Sean, was when he had an objective in mind. It was one of the few times I could tell their relation. Unfortunately for me, Byrein was more involved with his instruction than Mr. Sean ever was.

I stepped just outside and turned back to

Byrein, waiting for him to join. I was to walk at his side when we were walking. A step behind him was okay, occasionally, but a step ahead?

Never.

I learned that the hard way.

I felt as he placed a hand at the small of my back. The warmth from his palm seeped through the fabric of my dress. It made my skin crawl, but I smothered the urge to react to it. He guided me along the path we were taking with confidence and arrogance in his steps. I floated along beside him, like a ghost barely existing in the moment.

I knew his intentions with his hand on me while we walked. I could feel it in his power radiating on his skin, like an electricity. He was gauging the strength of my power. Checking where my power was residing. Checking to see if it had changed any due to our recent experiments. Though he didn't say, it frustrated him that it wasn't ever obvious to him. And I didn't offer him anything to help. I continued to pretend to be oblivious to his intentions.

Several Exes stepped out of our way, just as they had for me in the morning. Their gaze always low, with their head bowed out of respect or fear, or a mix of both. With each bowing Ex we passed, Byrein's pride and ego grew. I could feel it with how he held his shoulders as he walked. How he stepped more definitely.

He offered me a whispered comment here or there, usually judgmental about someone before him, or something in the Encampment. Though most of the comments were not directed to me, I think he just was saying it to break the silence between us.

I kept quiet.

My gaze stayed just ahead, never turning to him, never turning toward the others. I was numb and allowed my face to remain of stone. I watched the path before me change, riddled with more loose stone and fallen leaves. The air felt different, and the space grew quieter. We were approaching Byrein's experimentation area.

A familiar footstep approached us as we rounded the corner of the winding path. Their steps were confident and defined. There was a purpose in their approach, I could sense that with the minimal haste in their steps. I could also feel their power as they approached; then again, everyone here at the Encampment has power. This one, though, this one was specific. I only knew one other with this power radiating from their skin like a mist in the dark of night.

Renae.

It was Byrein's right hand man—well, woman. I had seen her presence in a Sight episode I had last spring, just before I came to join Byrein here. At least I think I did. My time here has made me question a lot about what I did or didn't see prior to coming here. It all feels a bit fuzzy, kind of like a distant dream.

She was a beautiful woman. Beautiful and capable. Capable of more than I think I wanted to know. More powerful than many others here. It made sense why she was often by Byrein's side. Her power made her trustworthy and loyal in Byrein's eyes. But she and I both knew that the power I possessed was greater than hers will ever amount to be. And Byrein himself viewed it that way.

I knew something else, too. I knew it the moment I met her. As soon as I found out her name, I was sure. This woman was Kasius's half-sister. I never asked. I never had to.

She occasionally would drop comments about her distaste in her old family. In her parents. How they acted. How they thought. And every once in a while, when she would mumble to herself thinking no one was listening, she would mention Kasius by name. Her mumbles were laced with the hope that one day he would see his potential, like she had. Hope that he wouldn't be afraid to explore the horizons of his power. Hope that he didn't fall for what thoughts their grandmother would try to fill their heads with.

Kasius was supposed to forget Renae's existence. His grandmother tried to wipe her from his memory. But here she stood in my presence. And I was required to interact with her. Every. Single. Day.

Most days, though, she didn't talk much to me about anything. I didn't mind. I didn't feel much like talking to others most days either. Interacting with others seemed like a chore. Especially when it came to interactions with someone you didn't see eye to eye with.

"Byrein, everything has been prepared for you — and Esmari," Renae assured.

Her voice wavered when she mentioned me. There was always a slight disdain lingering when she spoke the sounds of my name. Like they were difficult to say and bitter to taste.

"Thank you," Byrein nodded.

She flashed me a look as she stepped past me. No other way to describe it than distasteful jealousy. As much as she tried to hide it from Byrein, it was obvious to me. She simply didn't like me. Though, I'm not sure she liked anyone.

"Oh, and Renae?" Byrein called.

She paused and turned sharply back to face Byrein. If I wasn't mistaken, I saw a sparkle in her eyes when she gazed back at him. She always was eager to appease his requests. Nothing too big or too small. She never opposed him and always followed through.

"Yes?" she responded.

"We may be a while. Please make sure that no one bothers us during our training today. I don't want *any* interruptions today," Byrein commanded gently.

She nodded to him before turning swiftly and leaving us.

"Shall, we continue, my Esmari?" Byrein prompted, pressing a solid palm at the small on my back.

I stood firm, but my heart sank in my chest. I

understood what was in store for the day, and it wasn't going to be pleasant.

two

The sun was just setting on the horizon by the time I was returned to my tent. My veins ached from the use of my power today. I was drained and groggy. My throat burned from cold, dry air and dust. I sank into my chair and tried to quiet the thoughts swirling in my head, the memories from the day, all jumbled together. I tried to make sense of it all. I tried to process.

Byrein had invaded my mind during a part of

today's training, leaving a throbbing sensation at my temple for a good hour. He wanted me to learn how to do so, too, claiming how "useful" it was, and how superior it made us Mind Sights.

I hated it.

I always had. From the first time he had invaded my mind, to now with his instruction of the *art,* my distaste in the vile idea hadn't changed. But I didn't have a choice. Not here. Not now. Not in my position. I still had to learn the act. No matter my opinion on it.

It was worse than touching and connecting to someone's power. That part I was growing used to. And my general numbness to all feeling, at the moment, masked the craving for power. It just became a part of my day. Another task to endure and complete. Something to do and get over with, in order to survive another day.

But taking control of someone's mind? Speaking directly into their skull? I basically had to touch someone's power through the will of my own power. At the mercy of their pain. I knew the sting it would leave, and the crippling emptiness when the task was done.

It messed with my head too. Trying to sort

through the sludge of thoughts, figuring out which were mine and which were theirs. Figuring out what to speak into their head in a coherent sentence is a challenge all on its own.

As much as it disturbed me to say, though, it was growing easier. It takes me less and less time to initiate the steps. The process made sense and was becoming quicker to execute. And I was sure it was from the new powers I was forced to absorb in our little *experiments*.

I missed the time to just feel safe enough to explore with my power. A howl from the increasing wind outside vibrated in my ears and I stood to my feet stiffly.

Closing my eyes, I thought for a moment of where I wanted to escape to. I wanted so badly to place a bare foot on the ice-cold ground and launch myself into a Sight episode. I could just float away, to anywhere I wanted. Someplace warm. And safe. And completely and utterly undisturbed…

"Esmari—" Renae beckoned, stepping into my tent and allowing a draft of cool air to lick at my bare cheeks.

Turning to face her, I stifled a groan in my throat.

"Byrein sent me to check on you," she noted. A harshness lingered in her words.

I nodded sharply.

"Do you require anything?" she asked.

"No, thank you," I offered.

"Well, dinner will be ready in just a moment. You are asked to make your way there," Renae informed.

A nauseous feeling bubbled in my stomach at the thought of eating. I was thoroughly exhausted. I just wanted to be left alone. I wasn't hungry, though I rarely was at the end of a long day of training from the one and only Byrein. But today, the mix of a lingering ache in my head and the overexertion made me want to throw up.

I shook my head, willing the correct words out of my throat. "I am not hungry this evening."

"Thought you might say that. It isn't choice, however," Renae noted, looking my face over. I knew she was searching for any hint that I was planning to retaliate.

But for just a moment, I think I saw a glint of pity in her eyes. As if she knew just how tired I was. As if some part of her really did care and did feel sorry for making me go. Though the look quickly changed to her normal harshness with a flick of her wings.

"Millie?" Renae called.

"Yes?" came her voice from the other side of the tent flap.

"Please ask them to provide the ginger tea with lemon for Esmari. She has asked to have something warm this evening," Renae instructed.

"Sure thing," Millie affirmed. We listened as her feet shuffled away in the crunching leaves.

"If you are feeling ill, sip at the tea slowly and take bites of dinner along the way. The ginger will help," Renae stated bluntly.

Her flip-flop of her attitude was hard to understand. She reminded me of Kasius for a moment. Reading me like a book. Understanding what I may need. Not asking for affirmation about the matter but fixing an unspoken problem. It almost stung in my chest just thinking of him. But then every trace of him would disappear when her normal attitude returned.

With a quick flick of her head, Renae stepped back and pulled the tent flap back, motioning for me to exit with her.

When we arrived at the dining tent, Byrein was

waiting on us. He took one look at me and lifted a hand to rest on the chair to his side. I knew he intended for me to join him immediately so that we could begin eating.

The warmth from each of the candles perched around the tent provided a soft glow to the space. I gathered the skirt of my dress in the crooks of my fingers, lifting just enough to keep the hem from catching on the legs of the wooden chairs as I passed them. A cool breeze dusted my open collarbones, and I did my best to stifle a shiver crawling up my spine.

A thick aroma of meat and potatoes wafted through as a breeze brushed by. It was such a rich smell that it made my stomach churn. I was growing to hate this meal for how often we ate it. On the other hand, it was Byrein's favorite. *Probably why we eat it so much, Es.* I flicked an eyebrow unintentionally at my own thought.

"Something you care to share?" Byrein prompted. *Oops, I didn't intend for him to see.*

I shook my head and kept my stoic face, expressionless and cold. Swiftly, I sat in the chair beside Byrein, resting my hands in my lap. I offered him no additional interaction. He let out a hot breath, which was riddled with dissatisfaction, but soon was pulled into a conversation with another Ex at the table.

I gazed at the large round table in front of me, for once actually taking note of the details in this tent. I watched as the shadows danced in the candlelight from the parties sitting and conversing around its circumference. The occasional clink sound would break into the conversation as someone's fork would hit a plate, or a clank sound as a glass would be replaced on the tabletop.

All around the tent were more tables of different shapes and sizes, with more Exes gathered to indulge in dinner together. Some were laughing, others were in heated discussions about who knows what. The man I was experimenting on reading his mind this afternoon sat across the tent from us. He was slouched back in his wooden chair, with his arms crossed and dark circles around his eyes. He looked just as exhausted as I was and didn't dare to look in my direction.

I wanted so badly to apologize for his inevitable drain in energy. It was my fault. There was no hiding that. But I knew I couldn't do anything about it. I couldn't say sorry. Byrein would surely see me as weak. I couldn't risk it.

I felt a presence staring at me. As I took another sip of my ginger tea and forced a bite of potatoes, I canvassed the space once more, only to lock eyes with Renae. Quickly, her judgmental eyes darted to Byrein, then to his arm casually strewn across my chair arm, before ducking her head and shoving another piece of meat into her mouth.

I watched as a strand of her sleek, dark hair fell onto her pale cheek. The chatter of the room hummed in my ears. Carefully, I cut a piece of meat off and placed it into my mouth. I tried my best to chew at the tough meat without showing the look of disgust on my face.

All around me these people, these Exes, were happily enjoying the dinner. Not one person cared that I was here, miserable. They carried on with life as if this was okay. As if they didn't know how much of a tyrant Byrein truly was. They saw me day in, and day out. They all knew what purpose I served here. They all knew that at any moment they could be the next experiment for Byrein.

And they simply didn't care.

They were glad to be. Willing to sacrifice everything to grow his power. And for what? It was an answer I didn't think I wanted to truly know.

I felt like the murmurs of those around me were filling my head faster than I could comprehend. My face was growing warm. I tried to take a sip of the tea to calm my irritation.

How could they not see my misery? How could they submit to this terror of a leader?

I could feel a familiar sensation building. Someone—Byrein—about to invade my thoughts. Rip into my head with his words. I didn't just *want* to stop it, I *needed* to. I couldn't handle anything more. Not from anyone, and especially not from him.

From the corner of my eye, I saw his hand lift to run it through his dark hair, messy from the windy day. It slid through the strands and then grazed the side of his jaw. For a moment, his index finger lingered on the small scar on his jawline.

I couldn't take the buzzing sensation heading my way. Instinctually, I used my own Mind Sight as a barrier wall, deflecting his invasion. A ringing formed in my ears. I could feel a pressure against my power, but I didn't back down. I didn't give in. I couldn't handle it. An anger grew inside of me like a fire, burning deep and fiercely.

I pushed against his power. Pressing it back. Pressing it away from me. I felt the tension and frustration forming in him. He wasn't happy with me resisting. I couldn't explain why, but I just didn't care. He had put me through enough for today.

A little voice of vengeance whispered in my ear. I wanted him to know what it was like. The pain he was causing me. I could feel myself slipping into my rage. Frantically, I grasped for reason. For the ability to stay a statue of unforgiving stone. For any sort of numbness toward him. He couldn't get to me. Not here. Not now. Not in front of all his people.

Electricity jolted through my veins. I clenched my jaw, grinding my teeth together. I needed to leave. I needed just a moment to refocus myself. A moment to breathe.

The noise in the room seemed to get louder. I don't know if it *actually* increased in volume, or if I was just more irritated by it. More aware and agitated. My head was spinning. Exhausted from fighting his invasion. Exhausted from being present. Exhausted from being this little puppet of Byrein's.

The tension increased. The electricity inside my veins grew more intense. The room seemed smaller, more crowded. Were there more people who joined, or was it my imagination? I couldn't tell.

I couldn't breathe.

Sharply, I stood, my chair screeching back as one of the feet caught a small rock. The table looked to me. Byrein's eyes burned into me like the flame of an out of hand bonfire. I cracked my lips to say something, but I couldn't form the words. Stars twinkled before my eyes. I could sense a pastel glow around me. *Am I using my Sage Energy?* I could feel my full wings at my back, but I didn't know why.

I wobbled for a moment, standing. Stepping backward, I accidently left my shoe behind and caught myself with a bare foot against the cool ground. A surge of power left the sole of my foot as I scrunched my toes in a useless attempt to steady myself.

I forced myself into Byrein's dark mind quite abruptly and unplanned. It was like falling into a pit of emptiness. I didn't like it. It didn't feel right. I didn't want to stay. I felt like I was disconnecting from reality. Disconnected from myself. I pushed his power away from me. Away from my mind. Away from my core. Away from my thoughts. I could only muster one word.

"Enough!" I commanded through him. Rapidly,

I recoiled out of his mind, leaving his idle power behind.

My body felt weak. I could see Byrein mouthing something to me, but the ringing in my ears drowned out his voice. He looked upset. Maybe confused. I couldn't tell. I tried to look around me. The room was spinning. I felt my body dropping.

Suddenly, everything was black.

three

I opened my groggy eyes to find myself in my bed. I could tell I had lost time. I just didn't know how much time. I felt disconnected from my reality. I could tell it wasn't early morning, and the weather had calmed down.

Carefully, I sat myself up in the bed and canvassed the space around me for movement. A shifting figure caught my eye. Byrein's dark, soulless eyes caught sight of me and approached my bedside. I found the bedsheet and laced it between my fingers to give myself some sort of stability. Some sort of distraction. I feared what he would say to me, and I needed to be sure he didn't see my fear, no matter how tired or groggy I was at the moment.

Byrein stood for just a moment. It was the first time I think I had ever seen his eyes contemplating and unsure of his own words. He wrung his fingers as he observed me. I wasn't sure I wanted to know what all was going through his head, through his thoughts. It was as if he was waiting on me to speak first, but I didn't entertain him. I could handle the uncomfortable silence.

He couldn't.

There were dark bags under his eyes, as if he hadn't slept all night. I could see the power radiating from him. Wafting like a visible steam off the cells of his skin. He had more yet again today. He seemed jittery. I didn't know for sure, but it was likely why his mind seemed so clouded.

Byrein took a step to the side, adjusting himself as he grew more uncomfortable in our silence. I, on the other hand, observed. I didn't mind the silence. I watched his facial expressions. His movements.

His muscles twitch. His power emanating off him, how it danced in the wafting air. I watched for any change so that I could respond accordingly. React accordingly.

He finally turned sharply to me and took a step. His muscles twitched in his neck and his hair swayed on his head. I allowed a breath to release, so he couldn't sense my tension. I wanted—needed—him to believe that I was calm and at ease, even though I wasn't. Byrein's eyes darted across my features, I knew he was trying to observe me too. Unlike me, he was failing.

"How you acted last night was..." Byrein started. It was as if he didn't want to finish his sentence. He stopped the words in his throat and began again. "You were out much longer than I expected."

I offered him no response.

He nodded slowly and folded his hands in front of him. "What would you like to work on today, My Queen?"

Was he asking me? Since when do you get to choose, Es? It felt like a trap. I didn't want to study with him. I just wanted to exercise my power. In my own way. And I wanted to feel safe doing so. Without his presence.

Would he let me? I didn't know, but maybe it was worth a try.

Carefully, I took a breath. "I'd like some time for independent power exploration, alone," I stated. I watched his eyes carefully. I could tell he was considering. He needed more explanation and reassurance. "I feel that I need to explore my limits of the increase of my abilities, now that they are stronger."

It wasn't a lie. At least, not entirely. I had taken in additional power recently, and he and I both knew just how that altered my capabilities and expanded the limits of my Mind Sight. I wanted to explore these limits, without someone breathing down my neck the whole time. More specifically, without *him* breathing down my neck and judging my every move. I *needed* to, for my own safety.

I missed the independence I always had while working with Mr. Sean. Here, I felt like I was under a magnifying glass.

All day. Every day.

It was uncomfortable and stressful. Always strained. Always ready to mess up.

Byrein's eyes softened toward me. It took me by

surprise. Partly because he was always so harsh, and intense. But mostly because I was making a request, which usually would upset him. He liked to call the shots and be in control. But he liked to keep me satisfied even more. He wanted his queen content. Something I was finding to come in my favor.

"Okay, my Esmari," Byrein agreed. He paused. "But you will stay here in your tent. I don't want anyone disturbing you. And for safety I will have Millie or Renae sit with you."

I knew he didn't intend it for *safety*. It was to make sure I didn't leave. It was so he knew where I was. To keep an eye on me. I knew. But I wasn't going to argue.

I looked at him directly and nodded. "Yes, of course."

I offered him no smile. No further satisfaction. Not even the slightest twitch of my expression. He didn't need to know that I saw this as a little victory.

Byrein looked me over one last time as if he were admiring a prized possession. Reassuring himself that I was really there. Not just a figment of his imagination. A twinkle in his dark eyes disturbed my very core. It made the hair on the back of my neck stand.

For a moment, he tilted his head in thought. A stray strand of his hair fell out of place from the others. Something was racing through his mind. His dark eyes glazed over.

He was someplace else in his Mind Sight.

Suddenly, his brow flinched, and I watched a pulse of the power emanating from his presence puff out like a kettle releasing its steam. He turned sharply, noticeably uncomfortable, and exited my tent.

A moment of peace rushed over me. I allowed my fingers to unlace from the bed sheet. My mind danced eagerly, thinking of all I could do. All the places I could go with my Mind Sight. All the people I could see.

A memory of Jewel's face flashed in my head, then Kasius. My heart ached to see them once again. I wondered what they were doing. *How* they were doing.

I pulled myself out of bed. I flinched, feeling the aches of my body. My shoulder was sore, as if I had run into a wall. I took my hand and rubbed it softly. The feeling of a bruise forming and a faint recalling of standing from my chair at the dinner table came to mind. I didn't recall much else. The only conclusion I could come to was that I had fallen on it last night at dinner, likely when I had lost consciousness.

I smoothed the bedsheet gently, being sure to fluff the edging and cover the wooden base of the bed. A cool gust of air touched my cheek as a strand of my tangled hair slipped from behind my ear. I ran my fingers through my locks, untangling it as I went, and smoothing it down along the way.

Quickly, I took another glance around my tent space. I took a mental note of where things were, just as a precaution. It helped me know if someone had come, or gone, while I was in an episode. Though it didn't always help. Nor did it seem to always matter.

I sat myself on the ground, with my spine and my wings resting against the foot post of my bed. It reminded me of being in my dorm room all those months ago. I would give anything to be back there, instead of here.

I relaxed my mind and my muscles, releasing all the tension I held in my body and preparing for the lengthy Mind Sight episode I was about to launch myself into. My hands rested against the ground. I listened for little bits of sound surrounding me, and allowed all of them to fade slowly away.

I felt my power seep from the nape of my neck through my shoulders, down my arms, and trickle all the way to my fingers. Willingly, I released a surge of power and slung myself into a Sight episode.

Jewel's orange-red tips of her blonde hair faded into view, then her face.

She was troubled. Unhappy. Completely unlike her constant bubbly personality I often saw. There was stress and strain and worry behind her once-bright blue eyes. I could see the tension in her shoulders as they rose and fell with her breath. She was slouched back in a chair, one which I recognized from her parent's house. The warm light of a nearby lamp gave her cheeks a golden glow.

I wanted more than anything to reach out and embrace my old friend. To hold her tight to me. Instead, I watched.

Her hand lifted a paper I recognized. It was the note I had left for her the night of the Regal Festival. I recognized the blue ink on the paper and the letters in my handwriting. Right down to the small smudge on the top right corner of the creased paper. I watched as she pinched it between her fingers and played along the edging with her polished nail in thought.

"Es," she whispered.

Hearing her voice stung my ears. It was so pained. So weary. So many expectations. So many worries. So much hung on her shoulders. And I put it all there.

But her voice was so clear. Like a ringing resonating in my eardrums all the way through to my chest. I clung to the sound as if it were a final breath of air.

I wanted to pause time right there with her. I wanted her to know I was there. I wanted to reassure her I was okay. I wanted to stay with her. I wanted to apologize.

She looked tired as she glanced over the letter. There were dark bags under the eyes that stared at the paper. I could tell she wasn't reading it, just looking. Thinking. Contemplating.

She swallowed hard and folded the letter back the way it was. I wanted to tell her I was there. I wanted to communicate with her. I didn't know how.

Jewel reached to the small table beside her and lifted a cup to her lips, taking a slow sip. Carefully, she returned it to the table and swiped some of the condensation from the side. She played with it in her hand, stretching it through her fingers like putty. Her eyes gazed upon it.

I knew I could connect to it. I'm not sure how I knew, but I did. Just the way I did in my presentation for the festival. My veins ached with my Sage Energy. I longed to feel that connection. I wanted her to know I was there. I wanted to show her that I was.

But I could feel the need for the episode to be over. Like a calling back to where my body sat in my tent in the Encampment.

I strained to connect to the liquid in her hand. She stretched it and peered through it like it were a looking glass holding all the secrets of the world. I knew I only had one chance.

Like a jolt of electricity, I released a spark of lime green into the liquid laced between her fingers. I watched as it sparkled against her skin, flickering in the shimmery blush on her cheeks.

A gasp left her lips. Her eyes widened and she shot straight up in her seat, dropping the letter out of her other hand. She kept the liquid perched at her fingertips as she looked frantically around the room, attempting to find me. I knew she couldn't, but she tried anyway.

I had gotten my point across. I had made my presence known. I grasped to stay. I tensed, hoping I'd get to. Just one more moment with her. I wanted to be with someone familiar.

I knew I couldn't.

I watched as her shoulders fell in disappointment. But a glint in her eye showed a longing of hope. Longing for answers she knew only I could provide. She at least knew I was there, even for just a sliver of time.

I felt as she slipped away like a rope flinging out of my fingertips. Her wistful blue eyes welling with tears as she faded from view. I embraced the inevitable of returning to the prison I had put myself in.

I felt groggy and fatigued. More than usual. Completely drained. A soft fabric shifted on my shoulders as I straightened my aching back. A blanket had been draped across me.

My fingers ached from the cold. My ears and cheeks felt like ice. A growl from my stomach gave way as I allowed my eyes to focus on the dim candle lighting of my tent.

Renae shifted in the seat across the room, her eyes meeting mine. There was exhaustion spread across her pale face, no doubt from babysitting my statue of a body through the day. She lifted a hand to cover her yawn with the back of her soft fingers. Tugging at the sleeves on her arms, she broke eye contact with me. I could tell she was considering her next words.

"Your episodes seem longer than Byrein's," she finally remarked.

I didn't know how to respond. I wasn't sure I had the energy to muster a cohesive sentence, let alone a necessary one. All I could manage was a slight nod of my heavy head as I tugged the soft blanket tighter to my chilled shoulders. My fingers lingered on the fluffy fibers of the fabric, and I played with my nail against the stitching.

"It's chilly, I thought you might get too cold, so I put the blanket on you," Renae commented. She tucked a strand of her long dark hair behind her ear, untangling it as she smoothed it down, as if to keep her hands busy.

"Thank you," I breathed.

Renae bit her lip and leaned forward, resting her elbows on her knees. She took a breath and looked me over for a moment and I sat waiting to hear her next words. Were they going to be snarky? Judgmental?

"What's it like?" she asked, her voice quiet and unsure. In a way I never heard her speak before.

I glanced at her. Her dark eyes filled with longing and wonder. I paused for a moment, thinking of how to answer.

I heard footsteps approach the tent. Millie tossed open the fabric to enter my tent. She hesitated, locking eyes with me. Quickly, she bowed her head.

"Hello, Miss Esmari. Can I get either of you anything?"

Renae seemed caught off guard and embarrassed. As if she didn't want anyone to know her vulnerable moment, she straightened rigidly, but was at a loss for words.

"A snack would be helpful," I instructed.

Millie nodded sharply. She glanced at Renae.

"Nothing," Renae commented with a cold tone, waving her hand at Millie.

Millie took one more glance at the two of us and exited the tent. I looked back at Renae and took a breath. I waited until I knew Millie was out of earshot.

"To answer your question," I said softly, reaching for my necklace, "it's disorienting. I lose time. Sometimes, I lose a sense of reality. I don't always have control of what I see. It's a burden at times."

I'm not sure why I felt the need to answer her, but I did. Maybe I was feeling generous from seeing my friend. Maybe it was something about the genuine tone in her voice. Maybe, deep down, I thought that it wouldn't hurt to take a chance to be on her good side, because it might just come in handy someday around here.

She nodded, soaking in the information like it was liquid gold.

"I wouldn't wish it on anyone," I added softly.

I watched a fleck of gray glint in her eye as she flicked a look at me, almost quizzically. Her shoulders were tense. Unsure about our odd-natured conversation.

"Byrein is always so happy with his power. Proud even. You seem disappointed in having it at all," Renae stated.

"Byrein is—" I bit my tongue. *He's not satisfied or proud of his power. If he were, he wouldn't want more.*

"We look at our power differently."

Again, she nodded. "But, Byrein talks so highly of your potential. I can only assume that he means of you being a Mind Sight. You have capabilities that most of us around here can only dream of. At least you can be sure to keep your abilities," her voice trailed.

"Renae?" I prompted.

"Well, it's just..." She straightened herself. "You are a very valuable asset. Some abilities are more valuable than others. Mind Sights in particular are, because they are who can keep the control of our powers, or, when needed, modify others' power. They can make it better. Byrein makes it better or takes it in as a service to us. To rid those of an insufficient power."

I couldn't help but look at her face and pity her. *Oh, how he has brainwashed you.* I listened for a moment as I heard the light steps of Millie's shoes against the coarse grains of sand and crumpled leaves.

She tossed the flap of my tent open with her elbow, allowing a gust of cool air into the space before us. Her hands clutched at the handles of a serving tray, complete with a few options to snack on and a glass of fresh water. With a nod, she slipped between Renae and I to set the tray down with a clammer.

"Well, I think it's time for a shift change," Renae said definitively.

I gave a quick nod and watched as Renae left.

four

It had been days since I had seen Jewel in my Sight episode. Days since I had reached out to her and felt her stress. Days since I had felt her presence. And I was beginning to think that my mind was playing tricks on me. That my memory of it was nothing more than a figment of my imagination, embellishing the parameters of my pieces of memory with safe images to help me cope with my unfortunate circumstances.

Between the new power I was forced to take in, and the muddled, everyday events that I somehow endure, everything was beginning to feel unreal. As if I were just floating. *How exactly did I get to this point, here in this moment?*

Of course, I knew that answer, but I hardly could believe the outcome. It wasn't living. It was existing. And if I could make it through one more day, then tomorrow might be better.

Tomorrow always came, but it was proving to never be better.

I was beginning to lose hope in it all. Hope in seeing the other side of this. It was starting to feel like this was all that I was ever going to get to experience. Nothing more with my life. Just the monotonous tasks of my daily lessons filled with morals I am forced to have.

If the circumstances were different, I wouldn't mind so much. If I weren't a prisoner of my own doing, then this might have been a better opportunity to learn. More so, if Byrein wasn't the person he was, I would be able to learn and thrive, instead of endure and survive.

Survive. That's all I kept trying to tell myself. I

can make it to tomorrow. I can survive one more day.

All the extra power in my veins, altering the power I had originally known, was making my thoughts construed. If I had a choice, I wouldn't take any of it in. Not one ounce. There wasn't a sound reason for me to ever take it in. *You had to, Es. You didn't have a choice.*

I was beginning to wonder if that was true.

It didn't make me any better than Byrein. I was still inflicting pain. I was still manipulating power. I was still relieving someone of their power. And I would never see them again. I never knew for sure what happened afterward. I just knew that they were "taken care of." The very words made me cringe, and I tried not to imagine what that meant in Byrein's sick and twisted mind.

I never asked.

Survive. Don't ask questions. Just survive. One more day. Tomorrow will be better.

A rustle in the leaves at the ground brought me back from my very thoughts. Back to the movement I was mindlessly executing. Stepping. Walking. Breathing. Existing.

I strode just a step behind Byrein. Watching as

he stepped. Just a small movement in his shoulders, in the way he released the hot breath still lingering in his lungs, and I could tell exactly what he was feeling about any given individual as we passed them.

A woman quietly bowed her head as we passed, pressing her hand to her son's shoulders, indicating that he should do the same. He was uncertain in his stance, and young. His back still barren from any sign of wings. His eyes flicked from the ground below him to the dusty, brown shoes his mother wore, waiting for a signal that it was the right time to raise his head once more and continue on their way.

Byrein's shoulders tensed. He was dissatisfied in the encounter. No, that wasn't true. It wasn't in the encounter. In the individuals. The encounter, the exchange, brought him euphoria, knowing the impact of his presence. But it was something about them as we passed that made his step hesitate in place, and in turn, mine.

Just as they began to lift their heads and move away, Byrein's hand rose from his side, softly displaying his palm as if to ask them to wait. The gesture made my jaw clench as I awaited his next move. He turned swiftly, and the boy flicked a look up to us before immediately returning his head back, bowed down.

A sensation danced across my skin. It was sudden and unexpected. Byrein stopped them because of the boy, but even he couldn't feel the peculiarity of this boy's presence.

"You boy," Byrein summoned.

The boy and mother both rose their heads to respond. His lips trembled open, "Yes sir?"

Byrein softened his gaze toward them. It was manipulative and deceiving, but they didn't seem to notice his tactics. In fact, the woman looked proud, starstruck even to be in Byrein's presence, and in mine.

"You haven't gotten your wings? What is your name?" Byrein inquired.

"Velkin, and no, sir, I haven't," the boy answered nervously, brushing a sandy ringlet curl from his eyes.

"He's still pretty young, he may not get his wings for a while," the mother chimed, her vibrant green eyes sparkling with pride.

Byrein paused, looking them both over, as did I. I watched for what he was watching for. Listened to what he was listening for. And just when I had felt lost in the process, I sensed it.

Byrein must have too.

He lifted a sturdy hand and pressed firmly against the boy's shoulder. With a nod, Velkin flinched. A smug curl of Byrein's lip and I felt him release a surge of power. He sighed, as if dissatisfied with the boy, unable to connect with him. Unable to connect with the young one's power.

"Your wings will make their appearance soon," Byrein cooed. His greed and need to know just what they would offer strained in his voice. The boy didn't notice. I did.

The mother's vibrant green eyes twinkled with delight, as did the boy's matching eyes. There was wonder and excitement. Byrein pulled his hand away from Velkin's shoulder and watched pridefully at his subject's delight.

His confusion, though, lingered behind his pride.

I could sense his discomfort in the encounter, the inability to touch the boy's power just yet. He looked to my face, but only for a split second. As if he wanted comfort in me. I remained a face of stone, just as I always did. I refused to be his comfort.

It baffled me that he would even try his power on such a young boy without even his wings to show for his place in this world. But Byrein was only thinking of one thing, I'm sure. He wanted a head start on the newest solid crown addition. Even without knowing what he was reaching for, he craved to touch the new power that this young boy was bringing.

But there was a flaw in Byrein's process. There was a hinderance in his plan. And I feared I was the only of the two of us to know.

This boy was not like the other solid crowns. He was different from the other essential pieces in this game of Byrein's. Something about him as a whole set off my senses about power. It wasn't something about his power, or soon to be wings. It was quite the opposite.

The sensation I felt was not a lingering of where someone's power originated from. Where its core might reside inside of them. It was faint and fleeting, like the smell of a fresh orange tree in the afternoon breeze.

I knew just why it felt off. Why it felt odd. Why his presence set my senses on alert, and my Energy power prickling at my veins. It was because the young boy was not like the others.

Velkin, I feared, was going to be a powerless individual.

Byrein didn't have the clarity to notice just yet. But I did. And I worried for the innocent young boy's sake.

I paused a moment longer, watching the boy turn and be ushered away by his mother. She was excitedly whispering something to him. No doubt it was about the encounter that just occurred between us and them.

Byrein cleared his throat. "My Esmari?" he prompted, as if to continue on our way.

"Yes," I responded, allowing my legs to move in his direction.

Today, I didn't know where we were going. I didn't care. I just wanted to go through the motions of the day.

I had been here long enough to know the lay of the land. I knew where most paths led. Not all, but most. The paths that mattered. The ones that affected me and my day-to-day. The paths that led me to my own tent. The paths that led to Byrein's. The paths that were quieter. The paths that were less discreet than the rest. The paths that led to Byrein's experimentation area.

We weren't taking those.

Byrein led me to an unknown path. A path that should make me scared, but I had long since been numb to this type of emotion.

The ground at our feet turned from the forest dirt flooring, dusted with the colorful autumn leaves and remnants of fallen bark from nearby trees, to a worn uneven stone pathway, likely many years old.

The stones were not nature made. They were hand lain with care and precision. Placed with reason and purpose. The multiple shades of grays and browns of the stones were surrounded by a vibrant yellow-green moss. The sound of our shoes against the solid pathway echoed into the silent space between us.

Byrein's shoulders relaxed back as we rounded a corner. I felt the tension seep from my skin with each step further away from the overabundance of power I felt around me. Like a wave of peace which I didn't know I craved so deeply. The only presences I felt, the only power, were that of Byrein's immense, ever-growing Mind Sight resting within him, sitting at his very core, and the two guards who had promptly stopped by two adjacent trees, a few short steps back.

I allowed myself to release a breath from my lungs and watched Byrein carefully as we both continued the path. He pulled a branch back for me to pass and pressed his fingertips at my shoulder blade. If I hadn't known him, I would think of it as an act of chivalry. A supporting hand if I were to slip as I stepped around the branch. But his power lingering at the pads of his fingers was proof of other intentions.

I stood tall and strong, showing no sign of curiosity or discomfort. If anything, I tried to show a lingering discontent, even though everything in me was buzzing with warnings.

I had been alone with Byrein before, but this was different today. As we kept creeping further from the guards, in an unfamiliar place to me, I had no other choice but to comply.

His fingertips fell away from my shoulder and a sense of relief washed over my tense skin. I tossed a glance to take note of where he positioned himself next to me, unsure if he wanted me to continue our journey or wait for him to lead us. This was not the time to test him.

Not here.

Not now.

Now was the time to be submissive. Compliant. Survive.

A sparkle glinted in his dark eyes as he caught my glance. I watched his wings flitter subtly at his back. I offered no expression, keeping my body stoic and my wings still. He nodded and took a stride forward, continuing up the pathway.

The air grew slightly colder as I realized our raise in altitude. The path became a steeper hill, and, just as I began to feel my breath begin to strain from the increase, the path evened out to a rock plateau, overlooking the valley below.

All of the Encampment was visible from here. The tops of the muted-color tents, swaying in the breeze, were scattered below. I watched as the people flittered about their day, giving me the slightest reminder of Banshui's North District on a busy afternoon.

Though the same feeling remained. It lingered over the land. A disturbance of sorts. An uneasy feeling looming over the individuals floating about their days below. It was that feeling deep down in your gut that makes your inner voice tell you to leave. Turn back. To turn around and fly far, far away from there.

Yet, so many of these Exes knew no different. They lived in this discomfort. Maybe they had that hope still. Maybe Byrein gave them that hope, that things would be better. That the feeling was just *okay*. Maybe they didn't have that inner voice to listen to. Maybe they had ignored it so long that it just disappeared.

The very thought made my skin crawl.

Byrein cleared his throat. I glanced over my shoulder at him and crossed my arms calmly as if to hug myself and give a sense of security.

"Our Encampment has come a long way in a short amount of time," Byrein breathed, not exactly to me, but to boast and live in his own pride for a moment.

I found myself straightening my spine and standing tall and stone-faced. I adjusted my jaw and allowed it to unclench for the time being. A breeze caught the hem of my dress and flicked it around at my bare ankles. I stared forward at the way the breeze blew through the trees and made its way through the Encampment. It was free, like I wish I was.

"I regret not being the first to find you. I regret

not being the one to show you your true home all that time ago. You spent so long away from where you belong. This is all yours. Your home," Byrein nodded as he spoke.

A memory of his scarred jawline coming to view in my mind while my mom and I shopped in Sky Athra flashed in my head.

"This is where you will thrive. These people know that you are who they can look up to. With you here, with you by my side, we can achieve so much," Byrein continued.

I was uneasy with him. Afraid that if I made one wrong step, if said one wrong thing, he might just snap. I could feel his emotional instability as much as his radiating abundance of power. It put him on edge. Jumpy. Uncertain. Unpredictable in the moment.

"When Destimov, our previous leader, was here, he created so much with so little. He always told me how when the Encampment was mine to lead over, I could make it my own," Byrein reminisced. "Now, you and I can make it our own together. Just as Destimov told me all that time ago, I want to tell you. These people need guidance from capable Mind Sights like the two of us. This is our future. This, all of this, is your future, my Esmari, My Queen."

I clenched my teeth once more. *If it were mine, it wouldn't exist any longer. I would willingly lead them into ruin.*

"It is our duty to ensure their success. Our duty to rid the world of those who are not necessary," Byrein noted.

"You mean rid the world we live in from the individuals of insufficient power and without power," I commented.

"Precisely," Byrein's eye lit up with pride in my words. "You understand."

His gaze searched my face for an ounce of acceptance in him and his ways. I refused to give it to him. Like a statue, I refused to react at all. It was all I could do.

"It's more than that, though. Mind Sights have the responsibility of putting things right. To relieve individuals of pointless, meaningless power. Power that does not belong. Power that is hurting the community *as a whole*. We are responsible for making that right. Don't you see that, my Esmari?" Byrein sighed with satisfied pleasure.

I knew what he was intending in his mind. That

he felt the need to take power away from others to become more capable himself. He felt that some power was useless, and if he took it in, then it was being put to good use. If he manipulated it, the way he thought it should be, he was making it right.

Time and time again, he was blinded by his own capabilities of control. He couldn't see past it anymore. There was no big picture, not like he tried so hard to convince himself and others of. Just more power and more problems. He was never going to be satisfied, because he will always see one more thing to *fix*. One more thing that was his responsibility to "make right."

As more Royals, and Ex's had children, he would take it upon himself to make sure that their power was to his liking. To the way he believed it had to be. To the way that he thought would benefit the community. The power that didn't keep to his standards, he would have to make it right.

I knew what he meant.

But one simple phrase boomed in my head. It flooded me with an overwhelming urgency that resonated deep within my bones.

Like Byrein said, us Mind Sights have the responsibility to make things right. And Byrein himself was a wrong that needed to be made right.

67

five

I could have done it. I could have gotten rid of Byrein right then and there. I had the opportunity. We were alone. Not even the guards could hear us up on that overlook of the Encampment. Not a soul would have known.

I could have done it.

But, I didn't have a plan. I didn't have an escape. I didn't have a cover story. I didn't know if I was capable in the moment. What was my strategy? Where was my soundproof execution of ridding him? Where was my sad sob story to talk my way out of the incident?

I didn't know. I wasn't prepared.

Worse, he was beloved by so many. The entire community would have come next. They would have become an obstacle. An army. And I, their enemy.

No.

As much as the opportunity was there, more problems were there. I needed at least some of the community on my side before I did. Some sort of doubt put into place. Something more than my word. An outsider. A leader they were forced to abide by and bow to.

Without Byrein, they could turn on me in an instant. I needed them to see that I was just as much a force as he was. And that was going to take some work.

I had found my footing on keeping quiet and saying the right things to keep Byrein at bay. To prove my loyalty to him and his little *home* for me. But it was about time that I started to find some leverage. And it was about time I find my footing as authority over these Exes.

It was a fine line I was about to walk. Gain their attention. Their loyalty. Find a way to expose Byrein's instability. But I needed to tread lightly. This was, after all, his little kingdom that he controlled.

For days, I spent every spare moment thinking through different scenarios. I needed to know where to start. I needed to take control of my situation.

Everything revolved around the Exes in this Encampment. The people were the center. Whether they came here willingly from Banshui or elsewhere with their twisted morals, or if they were brought here and brainwashed to stay, it was evident that they were the center. The core of a terribly rotten apple.

My first step needed to be with them.

As much as I hated the idea, I needed to spend some more time with them. I needed to understand them. Byrein enjoyed ruling over them. I needed them to see me as someone they could level with. He was concerned with making sure they knew their place, that they followed him no matter what. But for me, I need the possibility of them on my side if it came down to it.

But the biggest question I was finding was, where do I start? And how do I do so without Byrein becoming suspicious or upset about it? I couldn't very well hide it from him, even if I wanted to. He would have to know. *If you don't tell him Es, he may become agitated about the secrecy. He might even lash out on you, or them.*

I sat at breakfast, barely touching my toast on my plate. I think Byrein mentioned something about the jam being a wild berry flavor. Of course, that was in between his ramblings of who knows what. I tried to provide a nod here or there to make him think I was engaged in his telling.

"My Esmari, I am afraid I have to meet with some others today. There have been some — *changes.* We will not have time for our trainings today." Byrein sighed, almost sorrowful, like he had broken a promise he made with me. It was music to my ears, though I tried my best to leave my face expressionless as usual.

Carefully, I took a breath and nodded slowly.

"What will you do today?" Byrein inquired. The way he spoke made my skin crawl. It was as if he was trying to be gentle and caring.

I thought for a moment, choosing my words

carefully. "I'd like to walk the Encampment. Maybe speak with some of the people living here."

Byrein glanced at me. I could see his distrust raging behind his pupils as they dilated. His jaw clenched. I knew he was drawing conclusions out of my simple words. I knew his malicious nature was gaining control.

I looked him dead on and attempted a peaceful, sure presence. "You mentioned how these people know they can look up to me," I started.

Byrein studied me. I could feel the anxiety burning in my throat. I needed to convince him through my words. Say something that would put him at ease.

"I feel I barely know of them. Like you said, this is my *home*. I feel like I should really get to know it, and the people I am supposed to lead." The words were bitter on my tongue. I was fibbing, straight through my teeth. I once again lied right to his face.

"I just don't want them to lose their respect in you. They shouldn't get too comfortable..." Byrein trailed off.

"I would like to feel more connected. You know the people you are surrounded by, I don't. I think this would be a good way for me to do that," I noted.

I kept my voice unaltered and sure, even though I was terrified on the inside.

Byrein nodded. "I didn't realize you felt a disconnect."

I wanted to test my stance with him. I looked him in the face while I spoke. "I'd really like you to respect my interest in this. Our original plans have changed for the day because of your meeting. I feel that this is a good alternative for me to spend my day. How am I supposed to lead people I do not know?"

He released a breath. *Es, you may have taken that too far.* I cautiously brought my toast to my lips and took a bite to avoid fidgeting with my dress on my lap. The crunch of the bread was enough to break the silence as he contemplated.

I replaced the toast onto the small plate in front of me and lifted a napkin to the corner of my mouth. I silently hoped he didn't see the slight tremor in my hand. I folded the napkin and tucked it under the brim of my plate and smoothed my peach-colored dress down onto my lap. Byrein stood from his seat.

"Have Millie accompany you in case you need anything out and about the Encampment today," Byrein instructed matter-of-factly.

I nodded, knowing she was there to keep an eye on me.

He started toward the tent opening, pausing by me. Carefully, he lifted a hand and placed it firmly on my shoulder. I remained a statue.

"Be careful," he cautioned. Swiftly, he took his hand away.

It wasn't a voice of concern for my well-being. Both of us knew that. He wasn't entirely convinced of my reasoning to get to know the Exes here. But he also didn't stop me. I had challenged him, just enough, and he stepped down. I don't know why it worked, but I certainly wasn't going to question it.

He tugged at the cuffs of his navy blue button-down and straightened his spine before continuing out of the tent. I watched as the tent flap fell behind him. A waft of air pushed past me, and I allowed the breath to release from my lungs. After one more bite of the now-cold toast, I dusted my fingertips silently and stood from my seat.

I fluffed the bottom of my dress around me, momentarily missing the ease of a pair of jeans and a sweatshirt. I longed for the comfort of a pouch pocket against the knuckles of my fingers that rested inside. It's one thing to dress up because you want to, or for a special occasion, but to be forced to wear fancy dresses every day because someone you dislike has decided it for you… Not as fun.

I don't feel fancy. Not in the least. I just feel like a display. Like a useless woman parading about the day, only here for Byrein and his followers to gawk at.

I stifled a groan.

I could feel my power eagerly burning for my attention in my veins. Instinctually, I flicked a spark to my fingertips and watched as the colors reflected around me, adding light to the shadows. I allowed the Sage Energy to seep through my spine and fill out my wings, listening to the subtle buzz as it spread.

Bracing for the cold breeze, I exited Byrein's tent and locked eyes with Millie. She nodded and joined me at my side.

"I am going to explore today. Byrein would like for you to join me. I want to get to know the people here better," I stated.

She looked at me quizzically. "Why the sudden interest in the people around here?"

"I just figure I should know who I am around on the daily," I noted, not waiting for another response.

Millie didn't dare to offer one.

I began to walk toward the commotion of the Encampment. Toward these people that I needed to find a way to level with. How was I supposed to gain their loyalty? All I am to them is someone they are *told* to respect.

A couple glanced my way and immediately flicked a look toward each other before bowing their head to me. It was forced. Uncomfortable. As if they didn't wish to make these gestures, but they didn't have a choice not to.

I felt feared. Not respected. Disgusting how big of a difference that was. Something you really don't realize until it's directed toward you.

I thought that now was as good a time as any to just speak first. Say hello. Strike a conversation. It was obvious they didn't have the option to do so themselves.

"Hello," I offered. It was forced and fake.

The couple glanced at each other and nodded a silent "hello" before backing away, removing themselves from my presence. I took a breath and pursed my lips in.

This wasn't going to be easy.

I meandered down the path, observing the commotion as I approached. There were more people than I feel like I was used to seeing. And everyone seemed to have their heads down, going about their days.

There was less of a chipper-ness than back in Banshui. A tension pressed against each of their shoulders. A couple of men marched their way through the space with purpose and authority, causing two women nearby to step clear and whisper to one another.

It was like a prison that these people willingly stepped into. Structured. Uncomfortable. Forced. Everyone knew their place and were expected to abide by it.

I walked with less purpose, hoping to not draw attention. A difficult task with our difference of attire.

They had on simple clothing. Pants and a shirt. Some nicer than others, possibly because of preference.

My eccentric peach-colored dress shimmered in the light seeping through the tree branches. The details glinted in the light with every step. The fabric swooshing as I walked made me stick out like a sore wing.

Some glanced my way, smoothed their clothes down, and bowed a nod to me, clearing out of my path long before I could offer a greeting. A woman snatched her child swiftly from the ground and scurried away quickly as if I were a terrible monster to avoid. Then there were some whose eyes glinted with awe at my presence, anxious to even be in my path, let alone be looked at or acknowledged.

All these people had a similar nature to them though. A certain flicker in their eyes. As if they always felt in danger. It was a hint of frantic nerves and a taste of awe hiding just behind. An anxiety that fueled their movements through the day and fear that gave them reason to act irrationally. It was as if that was their very purpose. Unsettling to be around, yet, here I was. Choosing to surround myself with it. Placing myself in their path of possible outlash.

I fluffed my dress hem once again to keep it from catching under me. Millie adjusted herself just a few paces behind. She was quiet, but I could feel her eyes watching me. Observing, studying, just as Byrein does. Trying to predict and understand my next move. *What is my next move? Maybe this is a lost cause, just like you, Es.*

My feet led me, but my mind and my brain were elsewhere. I felt like a lost cause. A silly display frolicking through the Encampment. With a sigh, I continued observing surroundings for something of interest.

A wind chime was dancing in the late morning breeze somewhere nearby. It was melodious and rhythmic. I followed my ears around the path, just past a large tree.

Quietly, I stepped up beside the trunk and listened. Just below the metal wind chime hanging off a low-hanging branch was a woman sitting on a tree stump flicking her fingers to and fro. She swayed along with the enchanting melody in peace.

Serenity emanated from the woman, and for a single moment in time, it was just she and I. Listening to the sounds. Calmly. Peacefully. Worry free.

I clung to the moment, grasping for any extra second I could soak in. I was unnoticed. It was blissful to be invisible once more. But I noticed her. I remembered her rhythm, her brown unruly curls that lay midway down her back. All of it.

I immediately realized just who she was. That I

had met her, well, sort of. Byrein spoke to her and her son, Velkin, just recently. He was still wingless. Byrein was interested in when he would show his wings, and more importantly for Byrein, his exquisite power.

Millie adjusted beside me, and I caught her eye. She was uncomfortable with the woman. How she didn't notice us. How she didn't greet me and bow her head in respect. I flicked her a quick look, warning her not to address it. I wanted another moment of peace. Another moment to be unnoticed and invisible. Another moment to just listen in tranquility.

The chimes resonated in my ears. I shifted my weight as well, wincing as some leaves crunched beneath my footing. The chimes suddenly stopped. The woman froze. Her shoulders tensed. She was unsure. Her simplistic cream-colored wings flicked on her back, showing the only sign of design which lay like a pinstriping in navy blue along the edging.

Finally, she turned slowly, standing from the stump. One glance at me with her vibrant green eyes, and she quickly bowed her head. I could see the mixture of nerves, anxiety, and cautious awe in her folded hands. She stood attempting to stifle the tremble in her arms as she wrung her fingers in front of her. Her eyes danced, watching her dusty brown shoes below her.

Stepping forward I took a sigh. *No more invisibility for you, Esmari.* Millie watched the encounter uncomfortably, cautiously trying to predict the woman's next move, as well as mine, I assume.

"Please don't stop because of me," I offered.

"I—Ma'am—Miss—" The woman struggled to find the right words and continued to look down. Her voice shook as she spoke, hoping not to say the wrong thing.

"Esmari, please. Call me Esmari," I greeted.

"Oh, no, I couldn't possibly. It wouldn't be right. Miss Esmari. Is it okay if I call you that?" she rambled.

"I'm no teacher," I half-chuckled. The way she spoke it felt too much like I was supposed to be instructing a classroom.

"Ma'am it is then," the woman said softly.

"If you insist. And what is your name?" I asked.

She flicked a look at me, shocked that I would ask. "It's Winona, ma'am."

"Hello, Winona," I greeted, offering a hand to

shake.

She blinked at me and cautiously took my hand and shook it gingerly, quickly releasing it and folding her hands once more in front of her. I could hear a breath release from Millie's lips.

"You have a son, yes? Named Velkin? I believe I—we—met the other day," I noted with a smile.

"Why, yes, ma'am, I do—we did—" Winona's eyes lit up at the mention of her son.

I offered a palm, waving toward the tree stump for her to sit, and I went to sit on a similar, nearby stump. With a huff, I fluffed the bottom of my dress. I turned my nose up at it as I did so. Winona perched herself on the tree stump, watching me carefully.

"Ma'am, I—I'm sorry—I didn't—" Once again she seemed scared of speaking.

I sighed, and watched her shoulders grow rigid. Of course, I knew why. Byrein often sighed just before he would reprimand others. His subjects and following. His guards. He did it with everyone, including me at times. In turn, it was something his disgusting guards and right hands learned to do. I knew that. I saw them do so on numerous occasions since I arrived. It was always an indicator that they were dissatisfied, but that was not my intention.

"Winona, I want to thank you," I said softly. "You helped me forget for just a moment."

"Thank you, Ma'am?" Winona questioned the words cautiously.

"Yes. I was able to enjoy your music. It wasn't being played for me, nor was it on display for me. I was able to simply exist with you for a moment," I spoke plainly.

"You're—welcome—I think," she nodded. She thought for a moment and wrung at her fingers again in her lap. "Ma'am—um—is there something you wanted?"

Her eyes pleaded with me. They were nervous. Uncomfortable. Scared that she was in trouble. Or that I would do something to her.

"I don't need anything from you," I assured. That was a lie. I needed a lot of things. Freedom was the very top of the list. But it wasn't what her words intended to ask.

"It's just, this isn't usual. Am I in some sort of trouble or—" she thought aloud.

I nodded. She was right. This wasn't usual. This wasn't how Byrein did things. "Winona, I just wanted to get to know some of the others around here."

She looked at me quizzically once more. The irises of her eyes glinted in the light with confusion riddled in their details.

"I know, Byrein thought it was odd, too. But I just have lived around all of you and realized I don't know any of you. I wanted to get to know the people Byrein is telling me that we are to lead," I tried to explain to her. "Honestly, I would just love some good conversation."

I slouched as much as my dress would allow back on the tree stump. Kicking out my feet in front of me, I relaxed. I felt safe with this woman. I couldn't explain why, but I just simply did. Maybe it was her motherly nature. Maybe it was because even though she were a mother, we didn't seem all too far apart in age. Maybe it was her general presence, which was overall less intimidating than most others here.

"Tell me about you, Winona," I prompted.

"Well, what is it that you would like to know?" she returned.

"I don't know. Um—I guess tell me about your family," I suggested.

"Okay, well. My son and I live here in the Encampment. His father was a man I loved deeply, but passed many years ago, when Velkin was a child. I don't have any other family, ma'am. Where I grew up, just on the outskirts of a little nothing town, where I met my late husband. We both discovered our power and gained our wings around the same time. You see, he was a hand on the ranch I lived at with a family who took me in when my parents died. They were never a family to me, but they fed me and sheltered me," Winona's eyes lit up with the memories.

She paused and glanced in my direction. I smiled and nodded to her to continue. She took a breath and nodded in return.

"Long story short, the moment I got my wings, the family put me out. They said that I was now mature, and it was high time I was on my own. So, the ranch hand and I disappeared together into the night. We discovered our power together. Mine was Air and his was Fire. We eventually married in a little unknown town somewhere along our way and a couple years later, we were expecting our Velkin. My husband's Fire got away from him once in a forest while he prepared our camp for the night. I lost my husband. But some people from this Encampment found us that week, too. They took us in. Velkin and I that is. They cared for us. They gave us the only true home I had ever known," Winona's shoulders relaxed some while she spoke.

"I am so sorry for your loss, Winona," I remarked.

"Oh, oh, I've spoken too much. I am sorry. You do not need to be sorry for my woes, ma'am," Winona quickly retracted.

"I was the one who asked. You just talked about your life. You didn't speak too much," I cooed.

"My son Velkin tells me how I don't need to share so much. He says that not everyone needs to know everything that sits on my mind," she smiled sheepishly.

"Not at all. Actually, it's rather nice to talk. I don't get that too often. Everyone is usually too afraid to speak around me. It's rather exhausting," I noted.

She let out a chuckle. Her face paused with thought as she looked at the sun high in the sky. "Ma'am, I know it's unusual to ask, but as we both have noted, this is quite an unusual encounter anyway. Would you like to enjoy some tea with me? I would be honored to make us a little something to eat and continue our unusual conversation."

I looked her over and smiled. "That sounds wonderful!"

I couldn't shake the odd feeling that I had walking the pathway with Winona as she led us to her home. Eagerness? Maybe. But with a hint of rebellion steaming deep inside my chest.

I tried not to let it show.

I found Winona's company comforting, in a way I hadn't experienced in my time here at the Encampment. Be it her demeanor toward me, or maybe the way she was actually willing to drop formalities and speak frankly to me, she was a breath of fresh air.

Her curls of brown hair swayed with the slight swagger in her steps, brushing lightly against her back and collarbones. Every so often, a curl would catch on her wing, then spring free with her next step. She walked with an attempt of formality, and I could tell she was growing more anxious as we drew near to her tent.

There were steps just behind us, which I recognized as Millie's, following along, and keeping a watchful eye on me. Curiosity riddled her as she followed, though. Some judgement, but definite curiosity. I don't think she knew what to do about my encounter with this unusual woman. Likely, she was also fearful of losing her position as my assigned helper for allowing this to even take place. But I could sense, somewhere in her, that she didn't quite care and was allowing the curiosity to fuel her motives.

We rounded a large tree that looked as though it had been through some tough years with scarring in the bark of its trunk. This forest seemed like a winding maze at times, but Winona was sure in her journey through it. A small pathway of smooth stones presented itself. The stones were all different in color and size, and it was evident that it was hand-laid with care.

It was funny. Not in a laughing kind of way, but in the irony. It reminded me of the pathway that Byrein and I had taken up to the overlook. Likely some of the same types of stones that were used to form that very same path, were used to form the walkway that we now stepped on. The very stones that led up to the tent of our destination.

For a just a tent in a forest, the space before me was welcoming. If I were just wandering the forest on a random afternoon, I would have never assumed that this was the home of someone led by such a twisted soul. Or that they were a part of a community that followed a man who was both cruel and terrifying.

This place felt safe.

Of course, I knew that all to be different. I couldn't let my guard down *too* much. But, similarly, I still needed to gain Winona's trust, as well as the trust of so many others here. *It's such a fine line to walk. Gain trust, don't lose what you believe to be true.*

I watched as Winona brought a hand up at her side and flittered her fingers, almost as if she were playing an unseen piano. She moved the air along the ground out of instinctual comfort, just the same way I would bring a spark of Energy to my fingertips. Her wings danced along with the petals on a wilting, white wildflower hidden among some fallen burnt-orange leaves.

"The pathway is so inviting," I commented, breaking our silence.

"Ah! Yes," she breathed. "My son, Velkin, he likes to go for walks. One day he found this flat rock and said it would be great for right at the opening of our tent. Ever since, when he finds a flat rock of some sort, he will bring it home to add to our pathway."

I smiled, reminiscing with her, as another breeze grazed my cheek.

Winona pulled the tent opening back and waved a hand as a silent invite inside. I heard a breath leave Millie's lips, likely nervous about the unknown location.

Peering over my shoulder to her, I flicked her a soft smile. "Millie, would you like to join us?"

She looked at me, then at Winona.

"That is, if you don't mind, Winona," I affirmed with a slight nod.

"Oh, ma'am, I don't mind," she said, shaking her head.

I looked between the two women. "After all, this is an unusual encounter." I shrugged, then added, "Why not shake things up?"

I turned back to the tent opening and meandered in. It was cozy and warm inside, much unlike the cool breeze we left to the outside world. My tired eyes adjusted to the dim lighting, and I took in my surroundings as the others joined just behind me. Winona came inside and quickly gathered a few things from the table. She swiped at the crumbs and nervously adjusted the two chairs. Looking around quickly, she tossed the knickknacks onto a small side table in the corner and snatched a footstool. She set it down near the table as an extra seat.

"Please, ma'am, have a seat. I'll go make us some tea," she noted.

I nodded to Millie, who perched on a chair facing the door. I took the other chair and slouched back, feeling the pressure on my spine and base of my wings instantly release. The seams of my dress pulled at my ribcage, and I could feel the fabric fighting against me. Part of me wanted it to rip.

Byrein would think that one of his following ripped it and would probably use them for his next experiment. I frowned to myself and adjusted my stature, so the seams felt less precarious.

Glancing at Millie, she was taking note of her surroundings. Her fists were balled up with the lap of her skirt tucked tightly inside. She caught me looking and nervously searched my eyes for answers. I offered back a calm, reassuring smile. It was so much simpler to feel at ease without Byrein breathing down my neck and watching my every move.

A chill ran down to the tips of my wings, as I realized he could be. He had every capability to watch me at any moment, and so did I. I didn't feel his presence, yet I wasn't quite sure all the time. *No, none of that right now, Es. Don't let those thoughts spoil your moment of peace.*

I looked once again at Millie. She seemed so frail, so innocent in all of this, just as Winona seemed, and I wondered her story. I wanted to know why she was here. Why she stayed to be bossed around by a brute like Byrein. Maybe she feared him. Maybe he held something over her head. Maybe she was threatened. Forced to stay. Maybe she didn't know otherwise. Just like Winona didn't.

No, couldn't be.

Millie looked frail, but she was smart. She didn't strike me as someone who simply didn't know better. Maybe she believed Byrein or one of his followers when they told her that they had a better life for her. Maybe she was in some situation that she was done wrong by non-Royals and the Exes found her in that moment. Or maybe she agreed with these people, these ex-Royals. Maybe she believed that the world would be better off without all the non-Royals.

Sadly, I believed that last reasoning more than any of the others. It, unfortunately, tainted her frailness in my eyes.

Winona rejoined us with some mismatched teacups and a handful of teabags. She carefully set down the cups in front of us, and sat just as carefully in the seat across from me. Her hands folded tightly into her lap. Her eyes glinted with nerves and satisfaction in company.

"I am sorry ma'am, I didn't steep your tea yet for you because I didn't know which tea you would like. I brought all sorts out to choose between. Some floral, and some with lots of spice. And this one here is a loose-leaf citrus tea, which tends to be on the sweeter side, but it's a favorite of mine," Winona explained. I could hear her voice waiver just a tad with her words. It was clear my being in her home made her anxious, but I couldn't tell if it was because she suddenly feared me, or because she feared Byrein. Likely both.

A faint memory of afternoon tea with Ruby from my hometown flooded my mind. It made my heart ache. Her red hair and flashy wardrobe which smelt of Hunter's parent's shop danced across my memories along with her voice, "a good day for the tropics, isn't it?"

I smiled. "I'll try the loose-leaf."

I reached a hand and suddenly felt Millie's hand stop mine. She nodded and took two strainers, scooped the tea into both, and placed the strainers into her cup as well as mine. *She didn't trust this woman.*

I watched the realization on Winona's face, realizing the same. She looked distraught, not in that she did anything, but in that she didn't consider how it might seem like she did. Her brows furrowed and she bit her lip.

"I, ma'am, didn't realize — it does seem a little

odd. I suppose you must be on high alert in your position. I didn't intend to—it just, I really like this tea and I thought it would be a nice treat," Winona explained.

"Winona, this is a nice treat. It smells delightful," I assured.

Without waiting for Millie to try the tea first— I knew if she felt she could speak freely, she would have had some words of frustration for me — I took a sip. I needed Winona to be more willing to trust me. And by offering my trust first, I hoped it would put her at ease.

I watched Winona, and eventually Millie, do the same. A pressure burned at my veins, and I released a small spark of Energy onto the tip of my fingernail to release some of the growing tension. Allowing it to dance along my fingers, I took another sip. The refreshing citrus flavor dripped down my throat. It would have been a flavor Ruby would've loved, though she would want just a spoon of sugar with it, I think.

Winona's shoulders relaxed some. Her breath and rigidness released. And then something else...

She smiled.

A small smile at first, then the grin grew wider

and wider. It filled her vibrant green eyes and brought a warmth to her rosy cheeks. Pretty soon that smile of hers became a slight chuckle leaving her lips.

I found myself smiling, too. Carefully, I glanced at Millie, who was studying our host carefully, observing her stature and her expression. Winona's fairly odd behavior was making Millie uncomfortable, which, for some reason, made me smile bigger.

"What is it?" I asked cautiously.

"It's just—I—sorry—" Winona shook her head and calmed herself down. She took a deep breath and gathered herself. "This is just *such* an unusual day! An unusual week!"

"I suppose so—" I commented.

"First, my son and I meet Byrein. My entire time being here, I haven't talked to him face to face. Sure, I'd see him here or there, but I generally talked with the others in town, not Byrein himself. And to have him address my son directly!" Winona continued. "Now, I have you, Miss Esmari, ma'am, at my table, in my very own tent! And what are we doing? Sipping tea."

I giggled. She was right, to her I was someone

who bumped elbows with the leader. Byrein wanted everyone to respect my ownership of them through his extension, something that was disgusting to even consider. He wanted me to be viewed in what he considered my rightful place, above them. Above the followers. High and mighty.

And yet here we were, a leader's partner and a follower, just drinking tea. Enjoying some causal afternoon conversation. It was something so simple, it was funny.

I looked again at Millie, who peered down at her teacup. She carefully held the handle and saucer just below, but hesitated from drinking. I could see a smile forming inside of her eyes, too. She was stifling it, I could tell, but the air in the room was mutual.

After we finally calmed our awkward giggles about the situation, Winona and I enjoyed some more easy and casual conversation. Talking about interests and other things. It was the kind of conversation where the meaning and the content didn't matter, but the feeling of comfort you got when chatting did. Millie didn't contribute much to the conversation, but I could tell she enjoyed the encounter as well by the time we were ready to leave.

Winona and I found our conversations over tea becoming a regular occurrence. Each time, Millie would join us, and each time, Millie would begin to add little bits to the conversation, until pretty soon it felt like just another day of three friends spending some time with one another.

Of course, I knew that was not true.

The reality of the nature was that outside of that tent we were a follower, a supposed right-hand to the leader, and an assigned help. But, I came to relish those moments that I could feel Winona's trust in me growing. She was letting her guard down more and more. She still called me "ma'am," but she was more willing to talk freely with me. More willing to orchestrate a conversation around what she wished to talk about, not just what I would. Less apologetic and spent less time asking for permission or forgiveness for what she wanted to say.

We would always have tea at her tent. For me, it was a momentary escape. For her, I felt it was needed to keep her safe. And to keep her from Byrein as much as possible. She didn't know that, and she didn't need to.

As much as I selfishly enjoyed a moment to connect with someone else, I also knew I still had a goal. A hidden agenda to the conversation. It lingered in the back of my mind. It danced across my thoughts as I would walk to meet Winona. It fueled everything in me, and gave me purpose to keep up the charade. I needed her to trust me, and if it came down to it, I needed her to side with me. And I was beginning to see hope in a possible outcome where I survive this whole ordeal, even if I didn't know how it was all going to play out.

Byrein was distracted lately, more so than normal. He said it was because of something that I didn't need to concern myself with. He would say it in such a manner that made my stomach flip. What was worse was it made him even more unpredictable.

Part of me wanted to know. Part of me wanted to have some insight as to what he had up his sleeve, and what his next move was. But that would mean I would need to pretend to go along with whatever it is. And I don't know if I was ready to do that just yet.

The good thing about him being so distracted was that I didn't have to worry about him looking into Winona. He didn't search me for why I went on walks and talked to others in the Encampment. I could tell Byrein was beginning to fall for trusting me.

I could tell I was calmer after my "walks," as Byrein called them. It was easier to deal with him. He thinks it's because I am "starting to feel comfortable in my home," and I want him to believe that, because little by little, I can see his guard coming down with me. He is becoming so much easier to manipulate back.

"You are quiet today, ma'am," Winona

mentioned handing me a tea cup.

"Just tired, I suppose," I noted.

"Byrein had her out late for some lessons yesterday," Millie commented.

"Ah," Winona breathed with a nod.

She didn't know much about the lessons I had to partake in, but she didn't like to talk about them, and I'm glad because I didn't like to think about them any more than I already was forced to. It was like an unspoken out-of-bounds conversation rule we held.

I adjusted myself and could feel the tight fabric from my stiff lavender dress pull again at my sides. The fabric was laced with scratchy thread that created a shimmer throughout which stretched down to the floor and down my arms in full-length sleeves. It bothered me, and usually rubbed me raw. I sighed, knowing how much my skin would hurt later that evening.

Byrein likes this dress. Too much if you ask me. He says he likes how there is no question where I stand among the others when I wear something as "elegant" as something like this. It's always the most uncomfortable of the bunch that he likes the most on me, and the most uncomfortable that he requests that I wear. I'd like to believe that it's just to torture me, but I'm pretty sure it's because they are the shiny and sparkly dresses. Maybe to him more shine means more worth. Maybe he was just too shallow to think about anything but something shiny.

I tried to think of something else.

"Winona, can I ask you something?" I inquired.

"Of course, ma'am," she agreed.

"Why is it that no one else wants to talk with me like you do? I mean, I try to say a simple hello, and they turn away and leave as fast as they can," I started.

"Well—uh—th—that's—" Winona stammered. She swirled the tea in her cup for a moment. Her fingers traced the bottom rim.

"I would like to get to know more of you. I just live around these people here in the Encampment and I barely know anyone. And I feel like they don't give me a chance to," I continued.

I could tell it was an uncomfortable topic for Winona. She was thinking through her words, hesitating to start a sentence. Careful not to say the wrong thing.

"I understand if you don't want to talk about this," I said finally after the long pause.

"No, no, I just—ma'am—you and I have been meeting together. All because of a chance encounter. I try to mention it to some of the others, but they don't want to hear of it. It's too odd for them. But, it's more than that, really—" Winona tried to explain.

"How so?" I pressed.

She sighed and set down her tea. The cinnamon-stained steam wafted into the air, swirling about before dissipating. I watched it for a moment, waiting for her to answer.

"You, Miss Esmari, ma'am, are a territory no one wants to touch. You are too important for most folks here at the Encampment. Byrein has made that abundantly clear. You are our leader, alongside of Byrein. You are above us. If someone were to so much as look at you incorrectly, you have every right to—well," Winona attempted to explain.

So, they fear you. They think that you are as fickle as Byrein. That your temperament is the same, Es. I took a breath of defeat. I knew that it was likely something along those lines, so I shouldn't be surprised. But to hear someone blatantly say it, made it different.

"Ma'am, I—I didn't mean to offend you—or overstep—" Winona retracted.

"No," I said kindly. "You didn't. I suppose I just

hoped that this was not the case. But you talk to me. You give me the time of day."

"Yes, but that's because you showed me a different side of you. Like I said, we had an odd encounter that day," Winona comforted.

I felt like crying. That wouldn't help the situation. I knew that. I felt like I was a small child again, just trying to learn how to interact with others and attempting to make friends. Hunter made that so easy when we were kids. But he's gone. He's not here this time. This time I am on my own. This time I am attempting to make friends with an enemy.

"What do I do? I don't like this being feared thing. How do I get through to them?" I pondered quietly.

Winona smoothed at the lap of her pants, then her shirt. Cautiously, she took a sip of her tea, returning it to the table when she was done. She gently folded her hands in her lap but wouldn't meet my eye.

"Miss Esmari, as Byrein has made it clear, you are to be respected. You are meant to be feared," Millie commented.

I stifled a frustrated groan.

"If I may speak freely about it all?" Winona

asked.

"Yes, please," I begged.

"We are supposed to fear you. Byrein, our leader, wants us to view you as our leader too. But—" she hesitated.

"But?" I prodded.

"Well, it's clear that he is the one in charge. In that, I just mean that—well—it's the way you dress, ma'am. The way that Byrein dresses is still of importance, he holds himself to a higher standard, you see. But you are dressed in fancy gowns each day. It makes you untouchable. Not relatable. It makes people here feel almost *too* beneath you. They don't dare be around you, or don't care to. Either way."

I contemplated what she said for a moment. *So, it all comes down to the ridiculous dresses? They all judge you because of your attire, Es. And it's all Byrein's doing.*

"So, what you're saying is that if I stop wearing these annoying dresses, then people around would be more willing to say hello?" I pressed.

She nodded cautiously. "Maybe not everyone, but I know at least a couple people would see you as less intimidating to say hello—wait? Did you just call them 'annoying dresses?' Do you not prefer wearing them?"

I took a breath. What I was going to say, I couldn't go back on.

Decidedly, I answered, "No. I don't. I think they are just plain absurd. Byrein is the one who has equipped my tent with them. My wardrobe, stuffed full. These ridiculous garments are impractical and uncomfortable."

I looked at Millie's face and then Winona's. For a moment, I thought Millie was going to choke at my disregard and display of disrespect toward Byrein to one of his followers.

Winona, though, surprised me. I fully expected her to be uncomfortable. I expected her to gasp at my ill words toward Byrein or ask of me to leave for fear of him. Instead, she sat, quietly thinking. She wasn't upset or repulsed. She was taking in the information.

"What a typical man," Winona finally commented.

Her words caught me off guard and I let out a surprised giggle.

"I mean, really? My late husband—mind you I loved him very much—he didn't understand either. Does he even ask you your opinion? That dress that you have on, for one, looks like one of *the most* uncomfortable garments I have ever seen. I can hear the scratch of the fabric from here!" Winona gawked.

"The shimmery threading through it makes me itchy and rubs so bad that I nearly bleed some days," I assured.

"It's true," Millie confirmed with a nod and a sip of her tea.

"Well, then, why don't you say anything to Byrein? I mean, he makes it known that you and he are to be equals. If that is to be the case, then you should be able to voice what you do and don't wear," Winona prodded.

"No kidding," I said, thinking over what she just said.

"You know what? You keep mentioning how you want to get to know some of the others around here. I know for a fact, if you were to stand up for yourself in this, some of the others will respect you in a whole new way. They would be willing to give you the time of day, or at the very least favor your presence. To be frank, I think a lot of people just see you as Byrein's helpless—" Winona caught her words. "I—ma'am—I fear I have taken that conversation too far. I may have overstepped in my words."

"Not at all," I cooed. "As usual, your free speaking words are welcomed."

Maybe she was right. Maybe I needed to step up and stand up to Byrein in this. I mean, it was a small detail, but this could be just the test for Byrein's trust in me. It could go very badly, however. But I needed to try something. And this could be just the thing to show Byrein my stance and my nerve once again. This might just remind him who I am. And this might just show his followers who I am too. I fiddled with the skirt of my gown, thinking through my next move.

"Millie, I may need your help in this," I mentioned.

Carefully I glanced to her. The tea paused in her hand, resting against her bottom lip. She was anxious about the idea, but not surprised. Gently, she nodded.

"Well now, that settles it," Winona huffed.

She stood with certainty and hastily made her way to the closet. Out she pulled a simple pair of gray pants and a cream-color button-up shirt. Tossing them over the crook of her arm, she gathered herself once again and walked to me.

"Please, for the love of wings, change out of that

over-the-top dress," Winona begged happily.

With excitement, I obliged.

———

I had managed to make it to my tent without Byrein's knowledge of my casual attire. All the while, Millie trailed one step behind me, wrangling the monstrosity that was the lavender dress. I almost wanted to leave it at Winona's or have an "accident" getting a little too close to a fire, but I figured that Winona may have to take the fall at that point. And then I wouldn't be allowed to go see her again.

My nerves were beginning to get the best of me as dinner approached. Part of me wanted to think of some story as to why I wouldn't be able to attend. Sickness sounded too unlikely, plus I liked to keep that one sacred in case I really needed to get out of something really horrid. Exhaustion sounded too silly and weak. And honestly, I just couldn't think of any other acceptable answer for Byrein as to why I wasn't in attendance. Thus, I had to go.

I watched as Millie stuffed at the skirt of the dress violently, to fit among the others in my wardrobe, just as I felt the presence of another power entering my tent.

"Byrein is requesting—well!" Renae gawked, staring directly at me. I could feel my face flush with terror and embarrassment.

"I—" My mouth opened to say something, but the words didn't come freely. Millie managed to close the wardrobe with a clatter.

"Clip my wings! It's about time!" Renae praised.

"Wait—you're—okay with this?" I questioned cautiously.

"If it means I don't have to watch you prance around in those dresses like you are all high and mighty, better than *some* of us, then, yes," she stated.

"I didn't—I mean— it wasn't my choice, you know. Byrein, he's the one who—" I tried explaining myself.

"Who made sure you had just what you wanted to wear at all times. Nice dresses to wear," Renae cut in with a roll of her eyes.

"No," I detested.

Her face changed. She turned to face me. "Don't blame Byrein, you wanted to look pretty, didn't you?"

I shook my head.

The realization set in. "Byrein made you wear

those?"

I nodded. "I've hated them since I came. I will not be wearing them anymore."

Renae looked to Millie and then to me. "Why now? You've been here months, why are you just now deciding to say something about it? To make a choice?"

I pondered on my own thoughts for a moment. *Because, Renae, I needed to gain his trust first. I needed to become one of you first.* "I have my reasons."

Renae paused in thought. "I'll see to it that you have something other than dresses to wear. Byrein will come for us both if it isn't at least nice and presentable."

I nodded a silent "thank you."

"Let's first see how he takes it at dinner, and go from there. If he doesn't like it, then I don't want any part of this. Millie and I will leave first. If you want to do something this bold against him, it needs to be your decision alone to go through with it. I don't want you dragging anyone else down, you know, just in case. Millie?" Renae confirmed sharply.

I couldn't help but smile as they left me to myself for just a moment. I wanted to see Byrein. His mood. I didn't know what to expect when I walked into the evening meal with him. My wings flicked at my back, twitching with nerves. Wanting to be exercised. I couldn't remember the last time I flew. Not just a small flitter here and there around the Encampment, but really, truly flew.

I wanted to wait a bit longer. As long as was knowingly acceptable. I savored what could be my last moments of freedom if this all went south. The feeling was uneasy inside of me. Growing more anxious with the seconds fluttering by. For all I knew, I could lose every ounce of my progress with Byrein. All his trust in me. Something as simple as a literal pair of pants could ruin me.

Then again, this could be the best decision I have made yet. This could be just the test to see how much leverage I had in this entire situation with Byrein.

My own skin was telling me that it was the right decision, though I think it was just bias to the soft fabric laying upon it. I didn't know how much I could miss something like a simple pair of pants and a comfortable shirt on my back. I felt more confident. Being able breath properly, and move for that matter, probably had something to do with that.

No matter if it was going to be a good or bad

outcome, my decision remained the same: I refused to step back into another one of those itchy, stiff-fabric dresses again.

With a deep sigh, I touched the ground and released a minuscule surge out of my fingertip. I didn't plan on going back on my decision, but I thought it might be wise to catch a glimpse of Byrein to know what kind of mood of his I was walking into.

To my surprise, the moment his face came to view in my head, I saw a calmness and possibly a slight amount of joy behind his cold eyes. It made my skin crawl. This was one of his most unpredictable moods. Was he actually calm, or was he scheming? Was he happy and joyful about something someone nearby has said, or was he in his own mind thinking of his next attack, already satisfied in another victory?

Only one way to find out.

His face faded from view. I stood and dusted my hands on the pockets of the gray pants I wore, allowing my palms to enjoy the feel of the fabric once more. I carefully tucked a hand into one of the pockets and lifted the tent opening with the other to exit.

My mind was racing with thoughts, all of which

I was trying to suppress so that I could have my full focus on observing. I needed to feel like I could react to anything and everything, at all times, as soon as I walked in to face Byrein. I felt unprepared, and my anxiety mixed with my power nagging at my veins was driving me crazy.

I tried to focus on my present being. Where I was standing. How the sand on the ground and the crunch of the leaves felt against the soles of my shoes. I walked with as much confidence as I could, even though I could feel the tightness of anxiety wrapping around my chest, suffocating my lungs.

It wasn't until the first person turned to me along my path, wide-eyed and confused, that the reality set in of what it was that I was doing. The reality of my decision. The sheer panic upon my choices was vibrating in my bones.

There are moments in life where you make choices. Choices that don't mean anything at all. And then there are moments where you know with absolute certainty that the outcome of the choice you are making is going to alter things in your life going forward. Good or bad. It was altered, and there was no returning to the way things were before.

This was one of those life altering choices. This

was my moment to put to test my stance in Byrein's eyes. Through a simple set of clothes. And I couldn't help but be nervous about it. I knew his temper. I would be a fool not to be scared right now, in this moment.

More and more people glanced my way, wide-eyed, before ducking their head in a bow and scattering from my presence. It was empowering. Though, I couldn't really understand why.

My destination came into view and that feeling of empowerment was slowly seeping from my soul. *No, Es. You need to walk in there with all the confidence in the world if this is going to work.* I took a shaky breath and entered.

As expected, all eyes turned to me. Byrein was the last to turn, or at least it felt like it. His body turned first, tensing as he did with his wings tightened to his back. Then his neck and head, and lastly his eyes, which flicked to mine. They were just as dark and cold as ever, filled with confusion and malice. I tried my best, as usual, to make him believe I wasn't terrified. To convince him that he held no power over my confidence. Make him believe I was distant and unfazed of his terror, even though I could almost feel my bones rattling inside me.

I felt like I was doing a horrible job.

His eyes hardened, obviously displeased in my attire, and in my choice to counter his desires. I could tell he was considering his words. I could tell he wanted to say something to me.

With a deep breath, I flicked some power to my fingertip and played it nonchalantly along my fingertips, allowing my wings to fill out behind me. The low hum of my Energy power buzzed for just a moment as it filled all the veiny cracks of my black wings.

The feeling of my own power comforted me. It was a reminder of just how strong I could be, both for me and for Byrein to see. In that moment, I realized just how much he needed to be reminded of my strength. Where my stance in all of this was. And how little he could control me.

I knew he wouldn't say anything outright to anyone. It would be a sign that he was weak. That he didn't control everything. I gave him the best warning look I could muster up, trying to tell him with my chocolate-colored eyes to fix his face before anyone could see just how vulnerable he looked. Smugly, I allowed a soft smile to spread on my lips, softening my cheeks as I watched him obey my warning.

In that moment, I knew I had hit the tipping point.

It had been such a struggle up to this point. Every moment. Every conversation. Every painstaking bite of the tongue when all I wanted to do was yell and scream and run.

But now…

Now, I had made my first stance for myself against his wishes. And thankfully, it had paid off.

I could tell he was fuming behind his dark eyes and withering ever so slightly in my presence. The look on his face reminded me of someone: his father. It was the same look Mr. Sean gave me when he discovered what I really was. The same fire raging in his eyes as Mr. Sean had when he had thrown me into Mr. Higgens' office.

Steadying my nerves, I walked through the space, straight to Byrein. I could feel eyes falling upon me, watching as I moved through the tables. I could feel their questioning, but there was something else there, too. A view of respect and acknowledgment.

It was the respect that caught me off guard.

As I passed, the conversations began once more

at a muted lull. I played with my power on my fingertips, allowing it to dance and spark from one finger to the next. I felt as it pulled and resonated off every powered individual in that room.

The brushing of my pantlegs on one another greeted my ears as I walked, and I allowed it to fill the sound in my ears. I could feel the soft shirt against my skin rubbed raw from the horrid dress I was in earlier that day, and it reminded me even more of what I was doing.

Byrein's jaw clenched as I joined him, visibly displeased.

"Good evening," I offered, satisfied with my presence causing such a commotion inside of Byrein.

"Excuse me, Miss Esmari," said the man Byrein was just speaking with. He bowed his head slightly and stepped away.

I lowered my voice to a barely audible whisper. "The followers will notice your distaste, which is clearly pasted on your expression."

Byrein leaned close to my ear, matching my tone, his hot humid breath laced with irritated words. "You changed your attire."

I didn't miss a beat. "Yes, I did."

He took in a deep breath. I gathered my next

words wisely.

"I thought it was time to show everyone just how strong your Esmari is. We need to show the followers that we are a strong team, together. Those dresses make me look important, but useless. We both know that I am so much more than that. The followers will respect your Esmari even more highly — they will respect the two of us even more highly if they see us together like this," I whispered confidently.

There was a change in his presence. It was softening at my words. I could tell he was thinking about what I was saying. But I knew there was still that nagging in him, reminding him that I made the choice behind his back.

"You and I are the only ones who have to know. If you play this right, you will gain more respect than ever before from your following. They will see us working as an unstoppable partnership together. You will be more important in their eyes because of this. Their trust in the two of us, together, will be stronger than ever, because they will see your Esmari as a force not to be tested. Not just a frail woman, but a strong leader at your side," I continued with an unwavering voice. I raised an eyebrow complacently.

His eyes flicked to me, and I could see a glint of satisfaction in my words. The greed for the partnership that his following trusted fully glossed over him. I could tell he was imagining the success of it all. He was convinced that he had won me over. Convinced that I saw this place as my home. My legacy.

I offered a subtle pleasure to fall in my eyes as I peered right back at him, but not in what he thought it was. No, it wasn't because we were winning over the following. It wasn't because the feeling of complete control over the Exes was setting in, like it was for Byrein. It wasn't the idea of working in tandem with Byrein as an unstoppable team.

That was all what was swimming behind Byrein's eyes.

My pleasure stemmed from something else entirely. I was pleased in the control of the situation with Byrein. I had taken a big leap. I had spent months just existing and surviving. But tonight, things changed, all because of a daring move. All because I wore pants. *Who knew it would all come down to pants, Es?* I almost chuckled at the thought.

I stood taller and more confident than I had in a

long time. I had Byrein wrapped around my finger, and he was a pawn in my game now.

The best part was, he didn't even see it.

eight

By the next week, I had a wardrobe full of new clothing, including pants and shirts. I personally met with the Encampment's tailor, a woman named Lou, who would create garments as requested just by a gentle touch of some thread. She was unable to change the thread itself into something softer, which I tried requesting on a particular button-down blouse she created, but was able to create a garment of a perfect fit.

I almost admired her skill, that is until I learned that Byrein had created her power to be such a way. She was originally able to manipulate only yarn and create with the use of a pattern. Knitting without the needles, as she called it. However, Byrein "fixed" her and "helped her see her full potential," as she said. She informed me that there was so much more to her power that Byrein allowed her to discover. So much more than just a simple tailor. The look in her eye was disturbing, and I didn't want to know just what she meant.

I walked into Byrein's tent, per his usual request of me joining him for breakfast. I shrugged off my overcoat, and while I was disgusted by the hands that created it, and the hands that enabled her to create, I found myself grateful for the warmth as the days grew increasingly cold.

Byrein was visibly unhappy this morning. His jaw was clenched and the way he grasped his mug handle was a telling sign. Then again, this past week he has been in an unhappy mood almost constantly. I'm sure in part it is due to me standing my ground, but I knew that wasn't all of it. He was conflicted about me standing my ground, but he was staying late and having meetings with his cohorts. Always at someplace I could only deem to be the "Planning Tent."

Of course, I couldn't be certain. And I didn't dare to ask. Not with his state of mind so fickle as of late.

He sighed disappointedly. Hot vexation seeped from his nostrils. Frustrations and discomfort, and more than anything, greed for power and control.

I perched on the seat across from him without a word. I solidified my face of stone and peered over at him blankly. I didn't dare show him emotion. Not sympathy, not pleasure in his pain.

Nothing.

Byrein took a sip of his cup and moved his attention to me. His eye glazed over as he admired me from across the table. Placing the mug on the table with a clatter, which he hardly flinched at, his shoulders slowly lowered into a somewhat relaxed state. I kept track of his unpredictable hands.

"My Esmari," Byrein breathed. "Today, I have someone special for you to bring out their full potential. They could be...great..."

He said it as if it were a gift for me. I knew he meant for me to experiment. My skin felt like electricity was dancing across it, raising every hair, and sending a chill through me. I tugged at my sleeve cuffs to touch the palms of my hands to stifle the need to shudder.

"I see," I remarked.

"You and I haven't worked with this type of power before. I have worked with something similar, but nothing quite like this. So… unruly…" Byrein stated with an air of awe in his words. "Your amount of power, between the two, your Mind Sight and your Sage Energy, well… I believe that you can harness the greatness in this individual. You will feel it too, when we arrive. Today, it will be yours."

Byrein made it seem special. Like it was going to give me glee to hear those words from his lips. Like I was supposed to be honored or elated about the entire scenario.

"It's more than that," Byrein continued. "It's not just one individual. It's two. Ah, I am getting ahead of myself. You will see. I don't want to ruin the surprise for you, my Esmari."

He wanted me to manipulate two powers. I looked at his face and understood what he was asking immediately. He didn't just want them manipulated. He wanted me to transfer and utilize someone's power for another to make them "better" in his eyes. He was asking me to sacrifice one. He didn't need to tell me so I could understand. I knew just what he meant.

It wasn't until we had arrived that it all sunk in, though. Not until the two individuals were looking me directly in the eyes. They looked honored, at peace with the decision at hand.

But what was worse was how they looked appearance-wise. They were similar. No, more than that. They were identical. Identical twins. All the same features, except their wings, which were reflections of their own individual selves I could only assume.

Both were tanned in skin, and dark-haired. Their golden-flecked eyes were embracing one another, for what would be one of the last times. Their clothing was similar in fit and the exact same color. But their wings were different colors. Both of vibrant feathers, but one shimmered with blue and the other with orange.

The two sisters were smiling. There was excitement, not fear within them, making me think they were either naïve to what would occur here, or that they embraced the opportunity, as so many others also did. I didn't know which was better in this type of scenario.

Generally speaking, I didn't try to think much about the subjects of the experiments I so often saw take place here. I didn't try to observe. I didn't try to understand, or reason with it in my own brain. I existed, and tried my best to disassociate from the entire endeavor. Pull myself away from it all, just so I could make it to the end of the day, to the end of the experiment.

But today was different.

Byrein was having me take over the entire experiment. It was new. Nothing he had done before. This wasn't just a lesson to teach me. It wasn't just for him to show me the ways of the Mind Sight, as they so often were. Today, he wanted me to fulfil something he was obviously not capable of himself.

This was my experiment from the start. It was going to test my strength, and it was going to test my loyalty to him. He knew that. I knew that. If this charade of me being here was going to work, this experiment needed to go well. No issues. No hesitations. Not even an ounce of doubt.

I thought back for a moment, on a memory so distant in my mind that it almost seemed like a dream I had made up. The moment I decided to come here. Byrein didn't give me a choice back then. It was the safety of others or this place. I chose. Every day since then, I chose.

But it seems that Byrein has since forgotten that. He has forgotten that he had to threaten not only me, but the friends around me. Those in direct line of association of me. They were the ones he was planning to sacrifice to get his way. To bring me to this place. To begin to win me over so that I would stay with him, by his side.

He has forgotten all of that in his egotistical pride.

To him, I am here, and he has won. To him, I have seen his ways and have submitted.

Here I was, trying anything just to survive this torture, so that maybe, just maybe, my life would change for the better.

"My Esmari? You seem distracted," Byrein noted in an almost comforting coo.

I swallowed and felt a nagging. Of course, he noticed. But my mind was elsewhere, and my Mind Sight was too.

"Yes. I need to clear my head before I commence in today's activity," I informed.

I didn't wait for a response. Swiftly, I turned

and sat upon the ground. Byrein didn't protest, even though I assumed he would. He stepped back, saying something of continuing the preparations for my experiment.

I needed to clear my mind of this doubt that was beginning to cloud my judgment. I needed to remember what I was surviving for. *Who* I was surviving to be with once more. And I couldn't help but feel the need to see them right then, in that moment. Something was nagging at my core and telling me that it was right and that they would be together.

I brushed a couple of fallen leaves aside and placed my fingertips along the dust on the ground. I felt the instant comfort that the granules against my outstretched fingertips brought me. I blocked out where I was, who I was with, and what my purpose of being there was. For just one moment, I was Esmari.

I released a surge from my fingers and allowed my power to guide me into the space it wanted for me. My mind went to Jewel, then to Kasius, and within moments, the two were before me. They sat at a table outside, under a tree. Jewel shuddered, Kasius looked distressed.

They were both tired. Worry left dark circles under their eyes. Kasius was a face of stone as per usual for him, but the darkness in his eyes was one I had never seen. He stared at the table before him, not seeing anything at all. Jewel seemed to be saying something.

I attempted to listen, but I couldn't make the words out. It was like they were just too far away. I didn't strain. Instead, I watched. I looked at their faces, their so very distraught faces. Faces that had been through turmoil and faces that deserved everything in the world. Their complete exhaustion and existence. I watched for as long as I could bear. I wanted to be with them so badly. I wanted to sit with them. To embrace their presence. I longed to be home.

Suddenly, words were becoming clearer.

" — she would be here if she could," Kasius said. The words came through to my ears as a whisper.

They were talking about me. I wasn't surprised. But there was such a disappointment and a diminished spirit around the two of them.

I saw Jewel nod. She spoke something more to Kasius, and I know I saw her lips say my name somewhere in there, but I didn't hear any more words.

I allowed it all to slip away and inevitably return to the realities of my current situation. I felt the earth beneath my nail on my finger. I felt the breeze against my chilled cheek. I heard the rustling of the fall leaves around me and soon the voices of the sisters I was meant to experiment on quietly speaking in a hush. Byrein sighed. I knew I hadn't lost much time, because he wasn't irritated with me.

"Are you now focused on the task at hand?" Byrein inquired with a tinge of snark behind his words.

I disregarded his tone. It wasn't worth getting into it all with him. I knew that. It wouldn't change the outcome of the day. If anything, it would make the entire experimentation even more dangerous than it already was.

Slowly, I nodded and stood, dusting my fingers on the thighs of my pants. His hand gripped at my arm in a way to force me up. My Mind Sight episode cleared my mind in some ways but clouded my thoughts in others. I knew that would be the case. I wiggled my arm free from his tightening grip, feeling as the mist of his power wafted away from me. Gingerly, I touched my fingertips to my necklace charms and gathered myself.

A soft sprinkle began to fall from the sky as if the clouds were crying for what I was preparing to do. They were holding the tears I no longer found inside myself to cry. I watched as the plops of raindrops fell upon the ground, turning it a shade darker. The pitter-patter was soon accompanied by rolling thunder in the distance which echoed along the trunks of nearby trees.

I knew I needed to distance myself from what I was about to do. Distance my thoughts and my feelings that were all sending off sirens inside of me. I knew what I was about to do was wrong. Horribly wrong. I knew it went against everything that I held to be good and right. It made me no better than Byrein and his following. But one glance in Byrein's eyes and I knew there was no backing out.

I wasn't doing it because it was right or because I wanted to. I knew that. I was doing it because I knew Byrein's temper. I could feel his irrational behavior as he seemed more and more impatient with me.

Going through with this meant that one of these ladies, whether they knew or fully understood it, would not see another morning. They volunteered from what I knew, so either way there was no saving them. However, not going through with this meant that I, myself, wouldn't see another morning. I knew that much to be true, too.

I took another glance at Byrein standing just feet away. The expression on his face was becoming more unpredictable by the second. He stepped closer to me, and I felt my breath catch in my lungs. I was terrified to look at him, and even more terrified not to.

He turned toward my ear and whispered, almost inaudibly, "You are the only one for this task, my Esmari. Am I to assume you are questioning this?"

His tone was becoming threatening once again. Byrein was questioning my loyalty. Questioning my place alongside him. *Was he seeing right through me?*

I steadied my voice and answered, "I am preparing for the task at hand. I want to do it correctly for us. No mistakes."

The words were bitter on my tongue, but Byrein sighed. He turned, allowing a slight curl to land on his lip. His dark eyes were glossy and distracted, as if he were looking right through my very core.

Just survive. One more day…

Byrein stepped away from me once more and I finally allowed myself to release my breath lingering in my lungs. I prepared my mind, distancing myself once more. I knew it was the only way to mentally make it through today. I knew I was killing at least one person today, if not two. If this whole thing went wrong, it could very well destroy me in the process.

The incredible power radiating from the two women before me was devastating and intoxicating. The hair on my arms arose at the possibilities I could feel within them. Something I was learning involuntarily through my experimentations and teachings of Byrein. I wanted to ask their names, but I knew that just made it harder in the end. Instead, I asked them their power.

One had the ability to make people see anything they wanted in the moment. A Sight. The other had the ability to make them feel anything of their choosing. An Inflictor. I could tell that the sister who was the Sight was by far the more powerful, and she would be the one receiving the new power. The ultimate illusion. To make someone see and feel their choosing. Happiness, pain, sorrow, complete madness... The possibilities were endless. It would give them utter control over someone else, that is, if this all went in Byrein's favor.

I had the sisters sit side by side with one another. Their faces were peaceful and excited. At least once, I heard each of them mutter how "honored" they felt.

Blocking out all emotions, I began on the task. My arm reached forward. My fingers lifted and I placed them gently against each of their shoulder blades. As if my power knew what to do, I was guided into the experiment.

I kept my mind blank and endured the disgusting feeling inside my veins every step of the way during the task. I could feel myself slipping deeper and deeper into a darkness. I grasped hard to any reminiscence, for a reminder of who I was. Any safe place within me. Anything other than that darkness.

The process was long and grueling. I knew very quickly into the entire experience just why I needed to do be the one to complete this, and not Byrein. I needed to sever the power from the one sister before it transferred. Byrein wouldn't be able to. At least not well. I had more power and more control, sadly. Which made me the perfect person for this.

By the end, my arms and veins ached, and my

body was fatigued. My fingertips felt numb from the general buzzing I felt with my power during these experiments. My whole body felt dirty, in a way that would never wash off. Like my very being was permanently soiled, the way I always felt after this.

But today the feeling was more intense. I looked into the eyes of the now-powerless sister. Her fire and passion for living was diminished. Her sister, now even greater in power than ever before, was fighting to accept and understand the bond of the two powers. Her soul was strong. She would live.

Not like her powerless sister.

The empty woman was asked to stand by Byrein and thanked for her sacrifice to better the society. It was only then that the reality of her decision had set in, and the reality of her death became clear to both her and her sister. Tears were shed, but they were proud and accepting for the most part, for they both knew there was no return to what they once were.

I wanted to be sick.

I held it together as I watched the woman be escorted away. She only managed a single glance more at her twin. Byrein spoke some words of encouragement to the sister that remained. I didn't register what they were. It was all fake exchanges anyway. Something about pride, maybe? Who knows. Who cares.

What's done is done.

Soon, the other sister rose and left the space. But there was a tinge of disappointment and fear in her eyes. I couldn't help but think it was because of Byrein. She looked back to me for something—hope, maybe? I stared blankly, offering her not even a smile.

Renae appeared in front of the woman, likely to escort her back to her tent. Her eyes met mine. I could tell she recognized the lady before her. She knew something was different. She knew that her sister was missing. Her face hardened, but she didn't say a word. Just a simple, minute nod of the head.

Byrein came to me. His face was different than before. Not impatient. Ravenous with possibilities swirling behind his dark eyes. His pride in me was unmatched. Schemes were brewing in his thoughts, I could tell.

The rain began to pour down over our heads and shoulders. The sky was overwhelmed over what took place here today. It was grieving because it knew I simply couldn't. I didn't know how anymore. I was numb. I didn't move. Not for a long time. Not even when Byrein was speaking to me. I didn't respond.

My hair was soaked and stuck to my neck and face. My clothing was drenched and dripped from the hems. I kept still with a face of a statue. Listening to the water splash on the leaves and create mud beneath my feet.

The only thing that was clear was that I needed to leave this awful place. And when I did, I was never going to do any of this ever again.

nine

I woke the next morning sicker than I had been in a very long time. Likely from the cold rain I stood in for over an hour after the experiment was done yesterday, but part of it was also likely from the mental stress the day held for me.

I had an intense fever that lingered for days on end. I was so out of it that I couldn't even keep track of what day or even what time of day it was. When I was awake, my head was pounding, making it hard to sit up, let alone eat. So, any recollection of time was completely out of the question.

Byrein came to visit me at least once, and so did Renae, though I don't think that either did so out of concern. I was more of an inconvenience at the moment, and I think they were judging just how long this would continue on for. Though my lack of sleep and food made it hard to think straight, too.

Millie tried her best to help me through. Blanket on me when I was cold. Fanning me when I was hot. Forcing me to drink water when I was moderately awake. As different as I knew our beliefs to be, I was grateful she was there to help. Even if it was an assignment from Byrein himself. I am almost certain she just hoped to keep me alive so that she wouldn't be to blame. Though some part of me deep down hoped that there was more to it than that.

The one thing that kept crossing my mind during all of this was that I had to get out. I had to find a way.

A plan.

An escape.

I couldn't do this anymore.

All the fake comfort from assigned help. All the unwanted attention from Byrein himself. All the lies about who I was just to survive.

I couldn't take it anymore.

I was hitting my breaking point with it all. Just when I thought I was getting ahead. Just when I was learning how to manipulate the game Byrein was playing. I found that I couldn't take one more thing. I was going to snap.

It's a scary thing knowing that you are facing your breaking point, when going through with all of it as long as I had. Months of it. *No, Es. You can't think of that, not now. Not yet. Fear and feelings will get in the way.*

A shiver ran through my spine. I felt miserable. I was hot and cold. I wanted a blanket on, while facing a fan. I was hungry and nauseated simultaneously.

A voice broke through the silence. Byrein's voice. He was saying words of concern, just loud enough for others, like his immediate circle of disgusting creatures, to hear. His voice was not sincere. I closed my eyes to avoid glaring.

What is wrong with me? My anger was getting the better of me. My frustrations and temper were surfacing, and I felt myself fuming, needing to scream or yell or cry. It wasn't like me.

I had been so good at holding that face of stone around him. So good at keeping my emotions hidden away on the inside, pretending I felt otherwise. But it was like my power inside me was stronger than before and making it hard to control my own emotions. *Was I beginning to go mad like Byrein from all the power he forced me to take in?*

Maybe it was just my fever still lingering.

Another voice joined the mix. Renae's voice floated through the tent. There was a hint of harshness, much like her brother Kasius had when irritated.

"Can't you see, your experiments were too much for her!" Renae whispered sharply.

I couldn't believe that she was defending me. Let alone against Byrein. It made me wonder what he said to provoke such a response out of her, the very person who looked past all his flaws. I heard him scoff. I could feel the tension in the air. Like he was a snake ready to strike, and she was right in his path. She didn't waver. She didn't flinch or step back, nor did she respond further. She stood her ground.

The exhaustion set in, and I drifted off to sleep once again, involuntarily. When I woke, I felt groggy, but finally well-rested, though my sense of time was completely thrown off. A flicker of a candle at the far side of my tent provided a warm glow. Renae stepped into the tent, casting a long shadow across the space.

I nodded to her, unsure how to greet her. Carefully, I sat up and attempted to smooth my hair down behind my ears. I allowed my feet to swing over the bed and touch the rugged ground below. My wings felt cramped on my back from my long slumber. Cautiously, I stretched them both out.

My power felt like it would escape from the bottoms of my feet if I wasn't careful. Not because I needed to release it but because I felt almost too weak to hold it back. My head swirled and my hearing felt muffled. I wanted to sleep more, but I wanted to wake up all at once. It was an odd sensation.

I wanted to say something to Renae, who stood lurking half in the shadows of my tent. The silence was uncomfortable. I knew she waited for me to gather my bearings before presenting me with anything to answer. Perhaps she didn't know what to say, either. Perhaps neither of us really wanted to speak.

The events weighed heavily upon my tired

shoulders. I knew what had occurred. I knew what I had done. I knew that I was done with all of this. I didn't want to continue this charade of being here willingly.

The face of the two sisters flashed in my brain. I shook my head as if to shake the memory from my mind. It didn't work.

"Hello, Renae," I finally offered.

"Esmari," she responded in a sort of greeting.

I didn't want to be here. All I could think about was how I wanted to be anywhere but here. I wanted to leave. I wanted to run. I wanted to get myself out of here. Go to someplace warm with actual, physical walls to keep the elements on the outside.

Every extra second was unbearable. I fought to hold back the tears welling up in my eyes. Why was it that her presence, of all people, brought me almost to my breaking point?

"What are you thinking?" she asked bluntly.

I didn't respond. I didn't know if I could. I wanted to ask her for her help. I knew that I wouldn't be able to get out of this place without some sort of help. Asking her seemed like the stupidest decision possible, but also the only one I could think of. I wanted out of here as soon as possible.

Maybe I was being too rash. I couldn't barely think straight, after all. My now-altered power, intense in strength from those who I stole theirs from, was clouding my judgement. I could feel that. It was the very little amount that seeped into my veins during the latest transfer between sisters that set me over the edge. I didn't know how to handle it. *Just breathe, Es. You don't know if you can trust her to help.*

I looked at her once again, my eyes dancing across her face, attempting to read every micro-expression to know how to read her. Today, she was taking pity on me. Today, she stood her ground with Byrein, and he stepped down. She was feeling confident. I could smell that from across the room. But, I needed more than that. I needed something that I could use to convince her to help me.

But, what?

My mind fell back on Byrein. The interactions between Renae and him. On the way she would look at him. The twinkle in her eye that she would get when he would ask any task of her. No matter what it was, she would jump at the task to serve him.

That was it.

"Renae, I need to ask something of you," I said cautiously, keeping my voice as steady and as low as I could.

Her eyes hardened. Crossing her arms, she shifted her weight.

"And I think you are going to want to hear what I have to say," I added as alluring as I could manage, though I am sure after my fever sleep and lack of bathing, I looked like a complete mess.

There was a hesitation in her. As if she didn't trust what I would say next. Honestly, I didn't expect her to. But the curiosity was nagging at her. I could tell she fought to be interested in it. Even giving me a half-scoff and a subtle roll of her eyes. But I had her. I knew it.

She took a sigh.

I couldn't tell if I was getting good at my look while manipulating the situation or if she was genuinely just that curious. It seemed too easy, but I didn't have the energy to care.

She glanced around the tent. At the corners. By the fabric sides. By the chairs around the space. Then, for a moment, she pulled the flap to my tent back. She looked around hastily.

"You there, yes you. Go get Miss Esmari something to eat," Renae ordered.

A muffled "Right away" came from outside the tent, followed by a few marching footsteps fading away.

"Okay, you don't have long. Talk fast," Renae instructed, a slight annoyance in her voice.

She moved a long strand of her dark hair out of her face with her anxious hands. She flittered her fingers and her wings, and I saw her eyes glaze slightly, as if she were seeing something else that I couldn't. If I wasn't mistaken, she was using her power on her own sight to give herself comfort. Whisking herself away to a familiar place. I wondered just how much she did that in her daily life.

"I need to get out of here. And I am fully aware I can't do that alone," I stated. I brushed at the sleeves of my sleep shirt while I talked. "But, you would be just the help I think I could use."

Her eyes widened as she took in what I said. Anger flooded her face. Anger and fear for the very words she was hearing.

"I know. About your feelings for Byrein. I know you don't like me. I want nothing to do with Byrein.

He could be all yours. If we play this right, you could be his right hand. His comfort. Without me in the picture, he would have to turn to you once again for everything."

She took in the words. I could see her face soften at the idea. But there was doubt still lingering behind her eyes.

"What you are asking me to do — what you are wanting to do — this could get the both of us killed," she said coarsely.

"I know. Byrein won't let me go. He would do everything in his power to keep me here as his prize. I never wanted to come. This — I wasn't given a choice. But I am choosing now. I can't do this any longer. These experiments. It's torture to me." My voice cracked. I bit my lip to suppress the tears welling up once again in my eyes.

Pity washed over her face. She knew what it was doing to me. She likely watched it with Byrein from the beginning, and now me. But Byrein chose it, I didn't.

"This isn't my home. It never was. It never will be. But for my survival, I pretended it to be my home. I am done pretending. I want to leave — I need to get out of here. If you help, you can get Byrein all to yourself. Think about it, you don't have to dote on me as he demands of you. Isn't that what you would want?" I lured.

Her expression changed. I knew I had her.

"That would be nice to not have to babysit you any longer," she confirmed.

"The sooner the better," I pressed.

She pressed her lips together in thought.

"This isn't the place for you. You aren't one of us. You never have stood for what we have. Byrein may be blind to it, but I knew from the start that you didn't fit," Renae commented. "We have to be smart about this, *if* it's going to work. Byrein's got eyes everywhere. I know. I'm one set of them. First, you need to get better. Go about things as if they have never changed. Better yet, as if you are stronger than ever. You need to convince Byrein and the others around that you aren't a threat. They'll slip up. They will give us the chance to get you out without a trace."

It terrified me just how easy it was for her to form a plan around this. She likely had thought about this. But part of me worried that when she fantasized about it before, I wasn't exactly participating. At least not willingly. It made me wonder if she had planned to get rid of me in her own doing…

Though the way she spoke about it made me discouraged. She implied that it wasn't today. That I had to pretend and put on the charade for a while longer.

"We will have to find just the right time. But the sooner you are out of here, the better," she confirmed.

I hate to admit it, but she's right. If I went now, I wouldn't get far. Plus, Byrein is already on edge about my lack of presence around him. I managed not to make a face at the thought.

"In the meantime, you need to figure out how to pack some things up without Byrein knowing—" she stated.

I nodded and shifted my feet against the ground. I was scared about placing my trust in her. She seemed convinced now, but would she turn on me? Would she reveal me and my plan to Byrein?

I was beginning to realize just how rocky this entire idea was. I knew just how two-faced she could be. How secretive and illusive she was. Flutters in my gut made me nauseous with worry that I may have put my trust in the wrong person. I had no way of knowing if she would hold up her end of the deal.

I just needed it all to take place before a better option comes along for her.

A sudden wave washed over me like a gust of autumn air. I could feel his presence. I could feel him watching.

I had become more and more aware of his presence when he was using his Sight with his more recent attempts. It was like the uneasy feeling you get deep, deep down in your gut when you must confess to something you had done wrong when you were a kid. That nervous moment that you know you are caught and there was no way out.

Smoothly, I changed the subject, giving Renae a look that I hoped she would understand.

"When are they bringing that food? I need to get my strength up so I can rejoin Byrein again tomorrow," I inquired snobbishly.

I flicked a spark to my finger, making it a deep red color. It flickered along my nail, and I soon allowed it to engulf my entire pointer finger, then my hand. I turned it back and forth, watching as it lit up my tent like a smoky flame from a bonfire.

Renae raised a brow and nodded.

"Yes, Miss Esmari. I will go and check on that

now." Renae bowed her head slightly and exited the tent. I allowed my power to snuff out from my hand.

Byrein stayed.

I could have called him on it. I could have let on to my increasingly good capability of knowing his presence. Of knowing when he used his Mind Sight on me. I had trained myself to know. To feel for every minute change in the air just in case it was him entering. His intensifying madness lately had me in a constant state of survival, like a never-ending cycle.

But then a thought crossed my mind.

He didn't need to know just how good I was at this. It was a chance for me to convince him further of my loyalty. For me to trick him to let his guard down, just that much more.

He knew how I was around him. How I acted around others. He watched my every move, just as I watched his. Waiting, understanding, and assessing.

But I knew just how irrational his thoughts were becoming. I knew what the greed for power was doing to his own mind. It clouded his judgment. He saw little irrelevant things as a threat to his community. It caused him to overthink absolutely everything and act on a whim. Just the way a little encouragement in my loyalty would elate him to no end and cause him to think he was winning me over.

I pretended not to notice Byrein's presence. I wanted him to think that after it all, the experiments, the changes, I was changed. That he had won me over with this little community of his following. That I was starting to be as insane as he was in my obsession for more.

I looked again at my hand and with a flick I released a puff of swirling Energy. I didn't suppress it. I allowed it to engulf my hand and soon my forearm.

I had to say something. Even just a whisper. He was listening.

"Look at what Byrein has given me," I breathed. The words were like acid, but I knew they would do the trick.

I watched as the flickering red sparks ignited my skin. As red as my anger and frustration of being here. As deep as my passion to escape and my insistence on survival.

Byrein's presence faded away, but I stayed watching the steady flow of my energy. My feet gripped the ground, and my legs straightened to bring me to a stand. It was as if by nature, or possible madness.

For a moment, I slipped into it.

It was as if I couldn't stop myself. I couldn't help but give in to the overwhelming craving. I wanted it. I couldn't stop myself. I didn't even try to.

With another flick, I watched my second hand become engulfed with the same Energy as the first. It flowed from my veins with such ease, covering my forearms. It lapped at my bent elbows. It danced on my skin. It hummed a familiar and comforting tune.

I brought my hands closer together. I wanted to merge the power between my hands, just as I tried to do so many times before. But this time, my power didn't resist.

Like a whirlpool, my hands were drawn to one another. Merging with such beauty. The sensation excited me when it should have terrified me. I could feel my veins pulsating from the vibration of my Sage Energy rippling through me. The crackling and popping as the Energy danced about was soothing to my ears.

I could feel my wings spread behind me, filled out and pulsing at the veins. They felt stronger than I expected for how sick I had been.

A red misty smoke emanated from me. It came from my arms as my power spread up to my shoulders. It was mystifying to watch it dance in the air's movement around me.

The swirling color spoke to me. It comforted me and empowered me. It inspired me.

With a pressing force, I flung my arms out and allowed the deep red sparks and smoke to rain down around me. They fizzled out of sight.

I knew deep down my power was aided by the power stolen from others. It was only then that I realized just what addition of power was doing in my body. What it was giving me. It was like an addicting amplifier for my power. Taken and severed from someone's very core.

But just for a moment, I reveled in the new strength of my power, being lost in its capabilities. And just for that moment I enjoyed just how powerful I possibly could be.

ten

My feet found all the crunchy leaves on the ground as I walked amid the chilly morning air. Every sound felt overwhelming, and yet the crunch from a dry fall leaf against the sole of my shoe felt comforting. Satisfying even. It seemed to drown out the rest of the world and purposefully disrupt my racing thoughts, reminding me to simply exist unapologetically for a moment in time.

The conversation with Renae occurred so many

days ago that I was beginning to think it was a hallucination from my fever, or a dream from my extensive amount of time spent either falling asleep or half waking up while I was sick. It was unnerving. But, the way she would glace at me when Byrein had turned away gave me a glimmer of reassurance that I hadn't imagined the entire ordeal.

I tossed the opening back to Byrein's tent and stepped inside just as my ears reconnected to the sounds around me. A hiss had left Byrein's lips, and it was directed at an individual I recognized as being one of his trusted inner circle.

"—betrayal. Such betrayal—" were the only words I caught.

My guard was up once again. I couldn't afford it not to be. His eyes were glazed over with destruction and terror. I didn't even know what it was that upset him, or what that man just before him had done, but I knew Byrein was furious. He was like an explosion waiting to occur at any moment.

There was a pause. Byrein's jaw clenched, and his shoulders were rigid. His rage was written across his body language, vibrating in every muscle in his body, and the man in front of him was in its path.

Byrein's dark soulless eyes turned to me. I fought the urge to step back in fear. Fear of his next move. Fear that I would be in the strike zone. I tightened my black wings against my spine, clenching their muscles like I would clench my jaw or a fist.

"My Queen, tell him! Tell him of his betrayal!" Byrein shouted. "Come!"

He demanded me to obey. My feet followed his beckoning, not sure that I had another choice. At least not one that I would safely come out from. I joined at his side, making sure that I had him in my peripherals.

The man's eyes looked shocked and confused. He ducked his face in shame. I could feel his power across his skin like a thin layer of lotion. It flickered like a mirage on a hot day. I refused to say a word for fear that it would be the wrong thing.

This was a man who chose to be an Ex. Who chose to follow Byrein in his ways. Who believed the same as Byrein. Who helped to terrorize those back in Banshui. A man who very well could have been a part of killing my best friend.

But in that moment in time, I pitied him.

Byrein swayed, instantaneously growing calm.

His rage released from his presence. I snatched a peek at his face and saw the distant look upon it. It was zoned and peaceful. The face of a man whisked away by his Mind Sight.

I wanted to know where. I wanted to know how long I had without his rage or his unpredictable nature. He wasn't watching me, I was with him. So where was he?

I wanted to tell the man to leave. To run far, far away. To save himself. But I knew that he wouldn't. One thing I knew about Exes was just how loyal they were. And even if he would run, I knew he couldn't get far.

I stayed quiet.

Byrein began to move again. Calmed now. More focused. More controlled. I couldn't tell what was scarier, his unpredictable rage, or his methodic terror. Byrein strolled around the man like he was simply an object in the room, his hand now tucked in his pants pocket.

"Good morning, my Esmari," Byrein greeted.

I nodded, unsure how to greet him without setting him off.

"How rude of me not to greet you, My Queen, but to demand something of you as soon as you entered. These individuals are so hard to please sometimes that it just drives me crazy!" Byrein let out a chuckle.

"I understand," I lied.

"Destimov, when he was preparing me to lead, told me that this would happen. That sometimes some of our people would betray us. That they weren't always as loyal as they make us believe. And we just have to set them right." Byrein spoke so calmly it made me want to shudder. I stifled the need.

He stood at the man's back and looked at me just over the man's slouched shoulder. His empty eyes twinkled with fake sorrow and complete greed.

With a swift movement, he jammed his fingers at the man's shoulder blade, and I felt as he ripped the power out of the man.

Every. Last. Drop.

Byrein's wings fluttered at the rush of new power now resonating inside his body. His face curled into an insane serenity and satisfaction. The man, on the other hand, reeled back and grimaced with discomfort. The mirage of power washed from his pale skin.

Byrein pulled away abruptly and the man

collapsed to his knees. Dusting his hands at a job well done, he allowed a content breath to leave his lungs.

"Renae? Could you take care of this one? Don't bother moving it right now. You can worry about that when we have finished our breakfast," Byrein summoned.

Without a skip of a second, Renae entered his tent. Her stoic expression was mixed with happiness and confusion. It was hard for her to hide the excitement she had to serve Byrein, but I could tell she recognized the man slumped on his knees before her, likely considering him a colleague and friend.

I felt conflicted. This wasn't the first time I had seen this from Byrein. But to watch him have such satisfaction. Such pleasure out of the task. It was disturbing and rattled me to my core.

These horrible-minded people, who followed a sick and twisted leader, were not even safe from their own community of people. They were exceptionally loyal to one another and their leader. But yet, they are not even safe from the man they trusted to lead them. Most didn't care and would chalk it up to how it was for the greater good; but then there were a few who would willingly carry out an order against a person they considered a friend.

Byrein approached and turned me by my shoulders to walk with him to the table set for our breakfast. He mumbled something about how I didn't need to look. How Renae would take care of the dirty work for us, because she's so good at taking care of it. I flicked a look back and caught a glimpse of her waving a hand. The man's face became dazed. She flashed me a glare, and I turned back in time to hear a crack and a thud as his body hit the floor.

I listened as she swiped her hands together, as if to dust off the filth from a difficult task. Without a word, she turned swiftly and strode out of the tent, leaving Byrein, myself, and the limp man behind.

"Ah," Byrein sighed deeply as he settled into his chair.

I perched just on the edge of mine, afraid to relax back. I watched his eyes dart from me to the food, then to the mug in front of him, and back again. It was as if he couldn't slow his mind down. Like he was jittery and jumpy. I unfortunately knew the feeling of new power flowing through my veins a little too well. But we had different reactions to it.

To Byrein, new power was satisfying and addicting all at once. He craved for more. He chased that feeling over and over. Byrein enjoyed how the power felt seeping into his veins and colliding with his own abilities. More so, the entire experience left him feeling elated and buzzing with contentment.

To me, it felt the complete opposite. Disgusting. Sickening. Nauseating. Like I wanted to run and hide, or throw up. I wanted to rip my veins right out of my skin. It drained all happiness from existence, making me feel dirty and overwhelmed. Even though I was accepting more into my body, I felt empty deep in my chest.

Carefully, I picked up a fork and tried to eat a piece of fruit. I did my best to block out the idea of the lifeless body lying mere feet from my chair. I felt the hem of my shirt, twirling it in my fingers. I didn't know what to say to Byrein that wouldn't set him off. I didn't exactly care to say anything to him, either. Not after what I had just witnessed. It was easier keeping my mouth shut than it was controlling the words that came out of my face.

Though sometimes, the silence sets him off too.

My mind was racing on just how swift of a job he made of the man, and similarly just how swiftly Renae carried out her part of the job. That man was one of their own, and just like that, they had no remorse for the man. Tossed to the wind like a leaf from the tree. He had said something that upset Byrein and pushed him over the edge, something I don't even know about. I was part of it. I allowed it to happen. I didn't stop it.

It makes me no better than them.

No, you are doing just what you must in order to survive. If you're not careful, you may be next. I took a breath and stuck a piece of overripe cantaloupe in my mouth. Swallowing hard, I set my fork down quietly.

"My Queen, you haven't hardly eaten. You can't possibly be done," Byrein prodded. "Was something not satisfactory? I insisted it must be for you."

I took a swig of water.

"Don't tell me you pity the traitor—" Byrein started, growing sharp and directing at me.

"No!" I cut in quickly.

His eyes were terrifying, and I wasn't sure just how willing he was to keep me by his side in that moment. He searched mine, questioning my loyalty and doubting my presence.

"The cantaloupe was overripe. That's all it is. It ruined my appetite for fruit," I commented, nonchalant, trying to brush it off and convince him it wasn't a big deal.

Byrein let out a yell in outrage. With one swipe of his arm, he threw the food off the table. If I didn't know better, I would have assumed there was literal steam coming from his ears.

"First, one of my own betrays me—I don't even get to have my breakfast, and I get word of his utter betrayal. His disloyalty. And now? Now, the food is not up to My Queen's standard. Is it too much to ask? To have a simple breakfast with My Queen. MY ESMARI! Can no one be trusted?" he fumed.

I wanted to tell him that it wasn't a big deal. That I wasn't upset. That it was just a piece of fruit. I knew he wouldn't hear it. He was too far gone for any sort of reasoning.

What was worse was that I was beginning to realize just how close I was in proximity of this full-grown man having a full-blown breakdown. Completely within arm's length. If he were to turn and open his wings, I would be bashed by them. He was going for the table. Glass was crashing and breaking. I was blanking out. Allowing myself to absorb the full picture of his outburst.

I wanted to run away. Get myself to safety. Or

at least away from him. I wanted to disappear. Be nowhere near the shards of broken glass and flying food. Be nowhere near this man who has lost his mind. I knew that I wouldn't be able to.

He was lurching in my direction. I knew it was only a matter of time that I was going to be in his path. He was so blinded with his own rage he couldn't see that. The power he took in was fueling his madness in a way I hadn't seen yet. It was as if he didn't have control. And as if he didn't want control. Every second that passed, was one second closer to me possibly not making it past breakfast. And since I knew running wasn't a viable option, I had to settle for the next best thing.

I had two choices.

One, I could attempt to talk him down. Running to find safety wasn't going to happen. But, if I could create the safety here, I would maybe be able to make it out of this. Maybe I could soothe him enough to talk him down out of this. Reassure him as his supposed queen, which he thinks so highly of.

Or two, I could fuel his rage.

"I was just looking to have a quiet morning. But this has been anything but that. We can't even rely on having a decent meal, it seems like. It's just too much to deal with. Don't they know just how much you do for them?" I egged.

It worked. He was falling into the trap. I could tell. His eye glinted with malice over my words. Like I had just given him the world.

"You do so much too, My Esmari. You deserve to have a decent breakfast at the very least. You requested fruit. I know how much you like refreshing fruit, and now my own cannot provide a simple request from you. I will not stand for this!" Byrein assured.

His anger was heightened but now redirected away from my presence. It was as if he were trying to protect me. To stand up for me. To do right by me.

He stomped out of the tent, mumbling along the way. I knew what that meant. I knew that someone else was going to be in his path this morning. I knew that Renae would have more to "take care of" and "clean up." I knew all of this. But I couldn't help but take a sigh of relief, knowing that I was no longer in his path, at least for the time being.

I shook my head at the thought of just how far Byrein has lost it. However, I realized just how peaceful I felt at the moment. Mostly alone. In his rage and desperation to avenge me and my breakfast, he had inadvertently left me to my own devices.

My power nagged at the nape of my neck. I wanted to suppress it. I wanted to use this time to plan or to escape. I wanted to find a way to further my preparations for the inevitable. But my power pressed more and more insistently, and I knew I wouldn't be able to control it this time, even though I wanted to.

I found my way to the safest space I could find on the floor within Byrein's tent. My back facing the siding, but my front facing the limp body, and further, the tent opening. Not that it would matter. Once I was within the Sight episode I was about to enter, I was completely vulnerable.

Not that I had anything to be fearful of. At this point, I was certain that there was no way I would be killed. Unintendedly hurt, sure. But Byrein wouldn't hear of it. The only one that would likely do anything to me was Byrein himself. And he was currently on his rampage throughout the Encampment.

I have nothing to lose at this point.

I sat crisscrossed and rested my folded hands in my lap, allowing my knuckles to just graze the ground. I tried to relax my mind, which seemed like it wanted to race on every thought, except launch into a Sight episode. The unsettling need to use my power mixed with my mind fighting me to relax into it was frustrating. It was like my body and power were opposing each other. Like my power didn't know what to do.

Maybe all of this new power inside of your body is making this hard, Es. I nearly grunted. I felt like I needed to relearn my body, my power. Like it was uneasy and always on edge. I used to easily relax into a Sight episode. Launch myself unwillingly, even.

Now?

I felt like I was forcing my Mind Sight to work with me. Demanding my body and my mind to obey me. I sat here trying to convince myself to calm enough.

Today felt like it was worse than ever. I had more power than ever before, and I didn't know how to handle it. I didn't know how to control it. Byrein was losing his mind, and if I wasn't careful, I would too. It terrified me. I could very well lose myself in a Sight episode. Lose sight of reality. Lose the ability to understand where I truly was.

I took a breath.

Es, you are not just any Mind Sight. You are a True Sage. You of all people are strong enough to take control of the situation again. I tried again to relax. But something still felt off.

I closed my eyes and sat in the silence for just a moment. I allowed the world to exist around me. I allowed my mind to race on everything and nothing, all at once. I was sick of fighting it all. Of fighting for my survival. Of fighting my Sage Energy and my Mind Sight to work with me instead of against.

I wanted to just exist.

Something was off, and I couldn't even place it because I had my guard up nearly all the time. I wanted to understand my Mind Sight. Again, it nagged at me. It pulsated at my nape, resonating down the vertebrae of my spine and up through my skull. I couldn't focus. I couldn't understand where to be. I tried to release a surge of power. I could feel my alone time fleeting before me. It was like I was being pulled by my arms in opposite directions.

That was it.

The feeling hit me and nearly made me say "ah-ha!" right out loud. I couldn't launch comfortably because I was being torn in different directions. My

Mind Sight was trying to pull me one way and then the other at the same time. It didn't know how to focus itself. It wasn't just that I didn't know what to do with all my extra power as it meshed with my existing power, though I am sure that didn't help anything. It was because there wasn't just one thing that my Mind Sight wanted me to see. There were two.

But how do I focus on one? How do I find the first path? Maybe I am thinking about it too hard. Maybe I just need to do, and not think.

I felt myself lifting into the space before me. Like water soaking a rag, I allowed my power to seep out of my knuckles still resting on the ground, saturating the space before me. I wafted into the start of an episode and felt as the two pathways pulled at me. I waited for one to present itself as the superior. To have the greater pull. And when that one did, I allowed it to carry me off.

And the experience was like no other.

eleven

I rejoined Byrein later that evening. It took me some time to find him once again. He had summoned for me, and then told absolutely no one where I should meet him, just that it was expected of me. And when I eventually did find him, I was afraid of interrupting his continued rampage that seemed to last all day.

I had never seen him like this, and from the look of his following, they hadn't either. They questioned him and his movements. They watched and observed from a distance as best they could. Some followers were fascinated by him still in passing, but in a sort of way you would look at an odd display now, not in the way you would admire a person, let alone a leader. Some of his closer circle seemed at a loss for words.

While we walked back from the center of the Encampment, where I eventually did find the lunatic of a man, he rambled on and on about how he needed for us not to join the others for dinner. How we needed to complete some sort of task ridiculing his mind. I wasn't sure just how true that was, because he walked on the direct path of the usual dinner tent.

He would pause at times, waiting for me to respond, then would promptly keep talking. I wouldn't have answered him, even if I had been given the chance. I knew him a little too well at this point, and knew just how his temper was, especially after this morning. Most of all, I knew not to test it by saying something he would think was wrong in his eyes.

My mind wandered on my episodes from the morning. I was drawn to Jewel, just as I had been so many times before. She was watching as Kasius signed a paper that looked important. She looked solemn and stoic as she peered past. Someone handed Kasius a garment, but that was all I could see before I was drawn away.

My second episode revolved around a familiar face that I hadn't seen in months. Mr. Sean. I watched as he sorted through papers in his office. His head hung low, looking across what seemed like messy scribbles on parchment. There was disappointment and sorrow in his eyes. I couldn't tell what for, but I was sure that as I was being pulled away, out of the episode, I heard the whisper of my name leave his lips.

I grasped at the two episodes.

On one hand, life was moving on without me. Kasius was signing for something that looked important. He was very obviously not in the academy any longer. It made sense. We all eventually need to move on from there and find our place in Banshui. We weren't always going to be students. But some little part of me felt like I was being left behind in the world.

On the other hand, Mr. Sean was in the same state as where I left him. Forever looking for a solution to bring his son back to him. Forever looking to fix what he believed to be broken because of him and his own doings. Nothing had changed there. He still had my name lingering in his mouth. He still didn't seem to have a solution for any of it. But he seemed disappointed in the information at hand.

It was unnerving just how little and how much things could change outside of your immediate world. Everything moves on with or without you. And that made me feel like a miniscule grain of sand of unimportance.

It was as if I were existing in a completely separate world from them. I felt disconnected from reality. Disconnected from myself. I had spent so long here just surviving, that it seemed like I didn't quite belong anywhere anymore. Even thinking back on my time in Banshui or my hometown of Athra seemed like a distant dream that didn't truly exist on my timeline.

Here I felt like I was just floating in a time that I didn't truly exist in, either. Unfortunately, floating in a time alongside of a madman I was now watching yell about the placement of a tree in a forest. It was hard to understand his ramblings, but

I am pretty sure I heard him say something about its placement not being suitable for me. Not entirely positive why, though.

What has your life become, Es?

Once we had finally settled for dinner, I found my appetite to be finicky. Not much sounded good to me and my tastebuds. The only thing I could fathom to eat was an entire plate of some sort of salad. I think someone called it "couscous." It was brand new to me, which added a little life to my night.

I adjusted myself in my chair and watched those around me. Most were keeping a close eye on my area of the table, but for once it wasn't because of my existence. It wasn't because of my silly display of a gown that Byrein would dress me in, or because they expected some sort of spectacle out of me to prove my greatness for some reason. No, today their looks were because of their great leader. The man himself.

Byrein.

He looked angry at virtually everything. Displeased in his surroundings. In this world that he literally created for himself. And yet he wasn't satisfied once more. He wasn't content or happy with his creation.

His inner circle of his following was beginning to realize the absence of one of their own. They were beginning to question their safety and their position at Byrein's side. I could see it written across the room as clear as day. They were beginning to question their great leader. The leader who so easily struck down his inner circle of followers. The leader who so easily led with fear. It maybe wasn't always like that, but it was now. And his following was taking notice.

These individuals around me were scared.

And just like that, I was realizing that when they glanced at me, they weren't looking at me the same as they once did. They were looking for a sliver of hope. They were looking to me to see if I was seeing Byrein's ways and his lack of morals. They were looking to me for some sense of security and balance.

Most in that position would feel honored. They would maybe step up. Rise to the challenge. Provide that hope they are looking for. Give in to their insecurities and want to help. They would maybe even look for a way to take over so that they could rescue these followers.

But I, on the other hand, had no desire to. If anything, I found it fulfilling to see these Exes scared and lost. And if anything, I wanted them to know when they looked to me, that I would provide them no hope and no comfort whatsoever. They didn't deserve it from me after everything that has happened.

It was as if I were watching the community about to implode on itself, and I got so much satisfaction knowing that it was just a matter of time before it happened.

My mind wandered, though, on a simple thought. After all this time, I still didn't understand these Exes. I didn't understand why they were the way they were. What was the purpose? If it were as simple as wanting to live in a place full of powered individuals, they had already achieved that. Why attack the Banshui residents who merely were going about their days?

I understood that the non-Royals were viewed as indecent. But why even bother with them? Why did these Exes look to someone like Byrein and follow him? More importantly, what was he leading them to or for?

There had to be more to it.

I could tell in the eyes of these followers, in these ex-Royals, as they sat before me eating their dinner. They were scared that their leader was unfit. That he wouldn't lead them well. That one wrong move and they no longer would live to see the cause fulfilled. But what exactly was that cause they were to strive to fulfil?

It drove my mind wild not knowing the answer. Not understanding any of it. Was this all just so that Byrein could have unmatched power? For what?

A splitting pain crashed into my head.

"What is my Esmari thinking about that has her so distracted at the table this evening?" Byrein's voice said, booming inside my mind.

I snapped back and pushed him from my mind. His voice. His breath. His presence. All of it. With a swift movement, I slipped my shoe from my foot and pressed my toes into the ground, releasing a surge of power. Simultaneously, I released a flick of red power to my fingertip.

I felt my fierce power seeping through my veins. Carefully, I chose my words to speak into Byrein's mind. I was prepared for the worst outcome.

Glaring him down, I seeped into his eyes with my power, entering his mind. I could feel as he winced within my forceful presence, but I didn't stop. With a confident decision, I spoke into his mind.

"Tell me what this is all for."

I pulled away quickly. Retreating back into my own head. I didn't wish to stay in his head any longer than necessary. Just long enough to get my point across.

I slipped my foot back into my shoe and watched as his sturdy hand flew up to his temple. Pain rifled across his furrowed brow. I knew Byrein understood my stance. I knew he understood my thunderous demand. Without a shadow of a doubt, I knew. My full wings flicked at my back with satisfaction.

A subtle smirk spread across his face. If I wasn't mistaken, it was pride in me. But mixed with disappointment. I couldn't quite understand it. It was deeply unsettling.

He leaned to me, resting his hand at the back of my chair. He opened his mouth and whispered, "The next meeting, you will join me."

The words chilled me to my bones, and I felt the power drain from my wings along with the blood from my face. I sat there realizing just what I might have gotten myself into.

twelve

I was told to wait at my tent. Be sure to be awake and ready to go in time for Byrein to "take me on a little date," he called it. It wasn't a date. It was to the Planning Tent. The place he always would run off to with all these followers of his to discuss who knows what that would always get him agitated beyond belief.

I had waited four whole days until he finally told me that I would be joining him to "understand."

He told me about how impeccably important it was. And how this was the real part of being a leader. He told me that I was finally going to see the difficult tasks of leading these people with him.

Byrein made sure to make me know just how good he thought I would do. How I would be an important asset to it all. How he was finally seeing me step up as a leader at his side and just how proud he was. His thirsty black eyes would always linger on me like a trophy he had won. It made my skin crawl.

"I wish you could have met Destimov. He would have been so proud of you, of us. Knowing just what power we had and what an incredible mind I brought into this Encampment would have made him very happy indeed," Byrein reminisced blissfully.

He seemed more levelheaded today than he had all week long. Like he had a decent night's sleep and a good cup of coffee to wake him up. He reminded me a bit more of the way he first approached me back in Banshui. Methodical. Sinical. Premediated in every move.

Honestly, it was such a change from his recent demeanor, I wasn't sure how to take it. It was almost more unnerving because I expected him to flip a switch at any given moment and change back into the unpredictable madman.

I found myself more and more curious the last few days. Curious about this place I had been trapped. Curious about the Exes' motives. Curious about how not to become like them. This place confused me. Part of me thought that now would be a good time to pick Byrein's brain about it all. I wasn't sure when the next time was that he wouldn't be a complete lunatic.

Then again, the questions and the curiosities could cause him to lose it in a moment's time. I decided it best to stay quiet and alert. Observe and process instead.

Byrein requested that we stretch our wings. Something that I found we didn't do very often, and I never really understood why. I watched as he spread out his broad wings carefully. The shiny black feathers glistened in the morning light. They looked striking and powerful. Mysterious even. Like they held all sorts of secrets, just below every last one.

Byrein wore a chiseled dark blue button-down top and some gray slacks. He looked professional and poised. Like someone I would expect to have a lot of potential money. Like someone you would listen to if they spoke up.

He requested that I looked a bit more put together. I think he intended me to dress up in one of the ridiculous fancy dresses by my own choice. Just to spite him, I also found myself in pants and a button-down. Though arguably, I did follow his order. I looked more sophisticated than usual with my hair brushed into a updo to keep it out of my face.

His disappointment in my lack of frilly gown when he came to gather me for our "date" gave me just a tad too much enjoyment. I tried hard not to show it. Instead, I played the oblivious role. I even adjusted my shirt a few times when he was admiring me just to lay it on thick.

I fluttered just behind him in the crisp morning air, hoping that he wouldn't ask me anything I needed to answer. I watched his wings carefully, adjusting for any small movement to keep me just far enough out of his reach. He would drift closer, purposefully might I add, and I would adjust so his hand was just out of arm's length.

His hair danced in the subtle breeze put off

from his fluttering wings. Though we weren't very high, I glanced occasionally down below to watch the leaves dance against the dusty ground in the shadows of our outlines. A man glanced up from what he had in his hands to catch a glimpse of our passing.

The world around us slowed down as if it were holding its breath. The trees grasped on a bit tighter, holding on to each dying leaf for a final moment before releasing them to float down to the earth below. It was silent, all except our breath exiting our lips and our wings keeping us flying. A feeling of longing floated along with us. And for me, a feeling of homesickness.

A ray of sunlight beamed through the trees adding a golden glow to the thin fog of the morning. It was like a painting. Serene. So full of warm, vibrant colors. I savored it as long as I could while we made our way to an area of the Encampment more secluded.

We approached the Planning Tent and landed just outside. I could hear a muttering coming from just inside its cloth walls. This tent was different from the others. Wider. More open. No flap to enter into from the outside world. It was surrounded by large trees and had a path made almost entirely of the fallen leaves.

We entered and a sudden hush spread throughout the room in anticipation and respect of the leader before them. Byrein allowed his wings to relax out along his sides, much unlike me, who found myself tightening them against my back as securely as possible. Byrein canvassed the room, shifting his weight and tucking a hand behind his back. His scowl spread across his face. I stood next to him, awaiting his next move and, in turn, the others in the room to respond.

Renae stepped forward into the light being cast from the world outside the tent. She didn't say a word, just allowed her gaze to fall upon Byrein's face. If I wasn't mistaken, I watched her eyes soften and her mouth twitch at a smile. *What did she see in him?*

"My Esmari will be joining us this morning. I expect her to be welcomed," Byrein finally commanded.

A few exchanged looks. Some didn't try to hide a grimace at the mention of my name. For the first time since I arrived, I felt unwelcomed. Most everyone through the Encampment had a general sense of welcome. A general consensus that I was to be respected, and if that wasn't seen from them, things would not go in their favor. Most people were quizzical of me but looked at me like an untouchable entity.

Here, in this Planning Tent, it was like all bets were off. I felt like fresh meat in front of ravenous animals. Some of the individuals around me were sizing me up. Assessing whether I belonged in their presence. I got looks of disgust and looks of confusion. A few looked at me with the usual respect, but lots gave me no regard.

Byrein walked me through the space before us. He greeted several of the others, who didn't return the greeting in my direction or even acknowledge my existence. I almost enjoyed being unimportant. Byrein was all business. He talked with them about this and that. The conversations were so vague it was hard to understand for the most part.

One man showed off a part of his power to Byrein while I stood to the side, trying my best to stay out of the way. I got nudged a few times, and I am pretty sure it was on purpose while Byrein wasn't looking. He left my side to whisper to another man, likely something I would rather not hear. And someone elbowed me.

I turned to see a smug-looking man with mop-like dirty hair hanging at his chin. He turned to say something to a woman beside him and I *may* have flicked a spark onto my finger and *accidently* brushed against his arm. He jerked toward me, just as Byrein rejoined my side. His wings drooped and he scurried to the other side of the tent, collecting some sort of materials.

Byrein leaned close to my ear, and I fought the urge to flinch or pull away from him. "Be careful. You are much more powerful than they are," he whispered.

I clenched my jaw, a bit upset that I had been caught in the act by him. But the glint in his eye showed his satisfaction. If I wasn't so revolted by Byrein, I might have felt a glimmer of happiness in the encounter and in the praise.

I took the opportunity to look around the tent while Byrein and another conversed. It was shadowy around the edges with little light, aside from what came in from the tent's opening. Along several edges there were long, uneven tables that looked like they would wobble if you leaned on them too hard. Papers were strewn about the tables as well as several small pencils.

Right in the center of the space was a large square table. It was sturdy and made of solid finished wood. It was sanded smooth on top and stood at standing height. Four large parchments sat rolled up in the center and a couple of cups there held some additional pencils.

Several Exes began to step up to the table, as if commanded by an unheard order. The large parchments were being unrolled. All except one, which was slid off to the side, out of the way. A mild glow presented itself from each as it was unrolled. One in blue, one in green, and one in yellow. The faces of the individuals reflected each color, making their skin look sickly, something I found to be quite humorous.

Byrein stepped up to the large table and motioned with two fingers at his side for me to join him. Cautiously, I obeyed. I stood, shifting my weight to find a comfortable position to be in. My arms felt wrong, no matter what I did with them, so I gently crossed them to give them a place to go and something to hold onto.

"Please update me on the progress we have been making—sorry, correction. Update *us*," Byrein prompted, nodding to me with a glimmer of pride in his eyes.

A rough man with a long scar across his eye nodded and spoke.

"Phase Two and Three are close to being set in motion. Phase One went smoothly and has set things up nicely in Region X," said the man.

It all sounded so fake. Like a made-up game with made-up language and made-up code. Like children playing pretend during their summer vacation from classes. I kept my mouth shut about it, though.

"And how soon do you think we can set the Phase Two into motion on this region?" Byrein inquired.

"I expect by the next full moon," the man confirmed.

Byrein looked over the glowing parchment. It all looked like lines and marks going different directions. There were some words scribbled on them that I couldn't quite read from my spot at the table. So, I stood, quietly observing.

"We also reworked the region to include a more suitable pathway," said a woman, whose hair looked like it could nest a creature.

Byrein waved a finger in the air as if to pause the idea for a moment. He scanned across the parchment before him once more, taking in its information. As I waited, I was beginning to grow uncomfortable. I didn't know what it was they were looking at. I felt lost and confused and out of place, and I'm sure I looked just that way, too.

Someone across the way glanced at me and whispered something into another's ear. The other person caught a glance at me as I shifted my weight uncomfortably. They nodded in agreement, looking at me with judgmental eyes. I pretended not to notice.

"I think we need to widen our radius and allow for more coverage that way, but Jay disagrees. He thinks it would be beneficial to add more wing power to cover the ground we have more quickly, to move through this phase at a faster pace. Faster could mean more chance for error. But the same could be said about changing the radius of our original plan," the man suggested.

"Why would we need to deviate from what was already agreed upon?" Byrein pressed.

"Phase One worked, but barely. If we want Phase Two to go smoothly, there needs to be a change. Just because it succeeded doesn't mean that there isn't room for improvement," the scar-eyed man responded.

Byrein leaned to me. "If you were trying to cover more ground, would you choose to add more individuals to cover the ground? Or allow for a wider radius and spread what resources you already have? More involved means for a quicker means, but wider radius would mean for more ground coverage in the same amount of planned time."

I didn't know how to answer. I didn't exactly know what it was they were talking about. I was answering blindly. On a plan that I was never a part of and didn't feel like I should be.

"Well?" Byrein cued.

I took a breath and picked the first answer that came to mind.

"Wider radius," I stated.

Byrein considered my words. "Why?"

"Because think of a fire moving across a plain. More involved in a smaller area means faster and could mean less safe. More individuals to get in the way of each other. Less efficient. More room for error. More minds could mean more conflict. And a shorter time frame could rush the next phases. A bigger fire in one spot going wrong could snuff itself out," I explained. The words came a little too easily. "However, a wider radius prompts for better success. If one spot on the radius falls behind or fails, the wider range of a radius will allow for more margin for achievement. A smaller fire across a larger area at a steady pace will do more damage in the long run."

I didn't know if any of that nonsense was actually true. But it sounded good and made sense in my brain.

Byrein smiled. First with his dark eyes, then his cheeks, then his lips in a smooth curl. Satisfied murmurs spread across the Planning Tent. Nods of agreement and understanding rippled through the individuals.

Byrein motioned for them to open the other rolled parchment which remained untouched on the table. As it opened just in front of us, it gave off an orange glow and I quickly began to realize just what I was looking at.

A map.

My eyes were not deceiving me. Byrein stepped in front of me and leaned over. I stood awkwardly behind him. I could hear him retrieve a pencil from the cup on the table and shift the parchment before him. He leaned further over it, and I heard the lead from his pencil scraping across the parchment. I didn't understand. I wanted to see. I wanted to know what kind of map, and what was on that map.

"My Esmari is right. Wider radius would be best for this next phase," Byrein praised.

I wasn't sure I was worthy of the praise, let alone if I welcomed it. My heart pounded as I waited to see what was just beyond Byrein's blocking body. To gain a glimpse of this map once more. To understand what it was that he was doing.

He leaned back, placing the pencil at the edge of the table and allowing me to take a look at his creation. His masterpiece.

"It's settled, then," he confirmed. "This will put us one step closer to cleansing Region X."

I could see the plains and valleys marked. It seemed familiar. The trees represented by colors smudged across the paper. A glowing orange ring swirling around an area. Then, as if my brain had reconnected, I began to understand the words written out in front of me. I watched as the glowing ring widened and met Byrein's sketch of an outlined

new radius. First crossing a creek, then a patch of trees. It engulfed a valley. Velrox…
Athra.

thirteen

I stepped back, trying to catch my breath. My mind was swimming. My face flushed. Thoughts of my hometown raced through my head. Ruby, the loveliest, wingless woman to talk to. My late best friend's parents and their clothing shop. Mr. Clove and his cooky class. My brother Bray. My kind parents. All powerless, non-Royal, and at the prowl of Byrein's following.

And I am the reason they are a part of Phase

Two.

It terrified me to even think about what Phase One was. I didn't know if I wanted to know just what that looked like. Just how much damage was caused; just how many lives were ruined in Phase One. It was sickening. And to think that I have now put my own family into danger of "cleansing."

I didn't dare ask what that meant, exactly, but I had an idea. My mind kept dwelling upon the words "Region X." It made my gut sink. *Just how many regions were there? How long have they been cleansing?*

Byrein stood tall. He seemed happy about this meeting. Like there had been progress instead of thoughts of destruction. I wasn't sure how to think straight. I wanted to scream out. I wanted to throw a tantrum. I wanted him to know that he was hurting some of my own. My hometown. My family.

I stayed quiet for fear of his temper. I had only myself to blame for this. Had I not come, maybe the outcome would be different. Maybe they would not have included my hometown. Maybe they would have just stuck to the original plan. Though that didn't make it any better. There were still individuals, towns, and regions that were subject to this "cleansing" of Byrein and the Exes that followed his command.

"Thank you for your help in all of this. We are moving forward to making this world a better place. Rid of those pointless, powerless vermin. I have even been informed that there are crawlers out there still," Byrein gawked shaking his head.

The idea behind the cleansing hit me like a ton of bricks. He was trying to wipe them from existence. I don't know why it surprised me. I should have understood what the Exes stood for. I understood in my gut what they believed. But deep down, I hoped that it just rested at the idea of non-Royals in a Royal community like Banshui. Not helpless towns across the area.

I suddenly realized that I was being given a very interesting tool. One that I didn't expect to be handed over to me freely. As scary and sickening as the map was, it was just that. *A map.*

I had spent so many days here trying to survive. Trying to figure out how to be here. I couldn't tell where the coast was from here. I lost my sense of direction months ago. It wasn't vital information. And with all the experiments and the added power, and losing track of time, days at a time, I couldn't even begin to think about what direction was what, outside of the Encampment.

Maybe that's what Byrein wanted. To feel so lost here that it had to be my home. I would be sucked in and stuck like a stick in the mud or tar on a pair of wings. But today he brought me along to the meeting. He brought me to see what the true purpose of leading the Exes was.

His mistake.

I stared at the map, trying to absorb where it was that we were. The Encampment was not listed. Probably for the best. In case this map fell into the wrong hands for the Exes, then they would be discovered. Their position, their cover, their security would be all gone.

But I could tell from a grouping of trees what our position was. It took me back to that day Byrein took me to view all of the Encampment. The purpose that day was to keep me here. To convince me of this home. Instead, it provided me with knowledge to escape this place.

I scanned the map and homed in on one thing: Banshui.

Little did Byrein know that today was just one more thing that helped prepare me to escape this wretched prison. I found the grouping of trees. I found the clearing that we looked over. I found the place we did our experiments. I took note of it all. I knew just what direction Banshui was. I knew where to run when the time came.

Whenever that would be.

I felt a feeling building deep inside my soul. A feeling I hadn't felt in a long time. Something that I had suppressed for as long as I could remember: *hope*.

It was quickly fleeting as I realized at just what cost that hope came. My very own unintentional contributions to the cause.

Byrein dismissed everyone and I watched as the map and the other parchments with the glowing scribbles were rolled back up. There was a mummer as everyone began to disperse. It was like a buzzing in my ears, becoming increasingly overwhelming.

I wanted air. I *needed* air. To think. To breathe. To process. My Sage Energy power was nagging in my veins. Byrein's eyes fell on me, and I tried to look stoic and relaxed. To ease the tension, I allowed my hand to release a swirl of power into its palm.

I played with it, rolling it around in my palm and allowing my wings to fill out behind me. I watched the flickers of colors rotate through without a care in the world and tried to ease my mind. Pull myself back together. Become alert and aware of everything and anything once again. I tried to push my thoughts of leaving from my head. I didn't want Byrein to see me distracted and inquire. I wasn't sure I would hold my tongue correctly and was afraid I might slip up and say something I didn't want to.

Byrein stepped just past me. Without a word, he glanced once again at me and then at the space beside him. I knew he intended for me to follow his lead once more.

"You have shown your greatness and your intuitive mind well, My Queen," Byrein praised.

I bit my lip and swallowed hard, keeping a furrow from landing on my brow. I continued to play with my power, allowing it to engulf my hand and climb my right arm. My feet followed without much thought, just a pace behind Byrein so that I could keep an eye on him and simultaneously keep him satisfied of my presence.

Byrein led us back toward the center of the Encampment. A few of his guards silently joined. The journey felt much longer on foot than it did while flying. I became distracted by my own power flickering on my arm. My mind wandered along with my feet as they mindlessly followed the leader. Slowly, I allowed my power to snuff itself out and my wings to return to a relaxed state.

A few others passed us by overhead as we walked. Byrein would mention something about them or the meeting we had. It was as if he were trying to strike up conversation with me. The way you would around a new friend you hardly knew to fill the void in the uncomfortable silence. I didn't contribute.

I knew that the events of the meeting were a lot for me to process and that my mind kept rerunning the picture of the map in my head, but there was something else nagging at me. I thought it was just my power again, except it was different. Something felt different about the air. And the closer to the main area of the Encampment we drew, the more the feeling became prominent, outweighing my own insecurities and worries.

A familiar voice echoed in my ears as we approached. It was soft but clear, rebounding off the branches of the trees around. A woman's voice, followed by a boy.

I listened as Byrein grew silent. His breath was

prominent. He grew tense, feeling the same thing I did. I sensed as his anger grew inside. His unpredictable temper was surfacing. It was bubbling up like a hot volcano ready to erupt and take out everything in its path.

My heart pounded in my eardrums from the anxiety of the inevitable conflict mere moments away. I felt as my ears grew hot, and my hands shook beside my body. My muscles tensed, tightening my wings against my back once again. My breath caught in my throat. I wanted to step away. I wanted to run. I wanted to hide. But I couldn't find the courage to.

Instead, I followed Byrein as he flung out his wings and hovered just above the ground, darting to the source.

We rounded the bend of the path to come face to face with a wide-eyed Winona, staring at her son Velkin. She clasped her hands over her mouth and gasped at the events unfolding before her. There was pride and fear locked inside her bright green eyes.

I watched as Velkin stretched his fresh wings, which looked of bent wires tangled upon themselves. They shone in the light of the late morning sun. He swayed from side to side, to show his mother, who now had tears welling up in her bright green eyes. Pride shone across his face as he looked upon his mother's, and I knew that would be the last time he felt like that.

Velkin turned and confirmed what I feared to be true many weeks prior, when I first met the young boy. His left wing lacked the copper smear.

This boy, Winona's son, was a powerless non-Royal.

Byrein landed with a thud. His black eyes were boiling with aggravation. Winona was frozen in fear, and Velkin was completely oblivious to his fault. He didn't understand. He didn't know he was powerless. And he was in Byrein's path because of it.

"You!" Byrein sneered, sticking a finger at the two of them.

Winona's face was white from terror. She trembled in fear and dropped to her knees. Velkin looked at his mother and then at Byrein with shock across his face. This man he had spent his life looking up to, who led his community, was turning on him. And the boy was too young and too naïve to understand.

"How dare you bring this horrible creature into our home!" Byrein shouted.

Tears streamed down Winona's face. "I—my—he's pure—" she stammered with a screech.

"PURE? PURE!" Byrein gawked. His voice echoed through the trees. The encounter was drawing an audience.

Whispers spread through the onlookers. Some were pointing at Velkin. Some at Winona. Others were watching Byrein for his next move. There was a general sense of confusion and fear in the air. No one knew quite how to feel and watched in anticipation.

Byrein didn't seem to notice the crowd. He was blinded with rage and hatred. His hand drew up and he summoned for the capture of the two. Winona shook as she continued to sob. She tried to reach for her son's hand but was yanked away.

Velkin was shoved to the ground. I watched the leaves puff away from his body as it slammed against the damp forest ground. He tried to sit up, but a man with stringy brown hair pressed a foot onto his back, crushing his wing against his spine. Velkin gasped and grimaced. His sand-colored ringlet curls flopped across his face.

I looked toward Winona, whose eyes pleaded for mercy for her son. She attempted to gather her breath but let out another wail. Her shoulders dropped, and the man behind her shook her to get her to sit up to his liking.

"How dare you! You fraternized with the enemy! This boy is not like us! He is powerless!" Byrein sneered through his teeth. I could see the veins in his neck protruding.

"No—NO!" Winona pleaded.

"Do you dare contradict your leader? I can see with my own eyes that you have lied since you arrived. You may have power, but this boy's father was powerless. He is not a solid crown. He is not pure! He is powerless!" Byrein seethed.

"His father had power! His father had power!" Winona cried out through another sob. The air around her swayed from her loss of control. Her emotions mirrored the unwilling release of her power. "He is pure! HE IS MY SON!"

My arms burned and I looked down to see them engulfed in swirling Energy. I was livid at the display and petrified to move all at once. I watched as a subtle red smoke wafted from my fingertips and swayed around me.

Byrein moved closer to the boy and his mother. Gasps rippled through the crowd of onlookers. The commotion of uncomfortable shifting feet tainted the space as they observed their leader approach one of their own. His arms glistened with sweat, and his muscles contracted as he gripped his hands into fists.

I crouched down, watching in shock as the entire moment began to move in slow motion. There was a ringing in my ears, and I gulped for air to enter my lungs. I could feel the tension in the crowd and read Byrein's name on several lips. My heart thudded inside my head.

Byrein reeled back and I gripped at the floor. I wanted to stop him. This wasn't right. His hands gripped the boy's head full of curls and he yanked him to his knees. My eyes met Winona's and watched the air around her twist and turn, pulling the fallen leaves back and forth.

The boy's eyes met Byrein's, pleading for mercy. Byrein was too far gone for the boy to have any hope. A tear rolled down Velkin's face.

My mind was racing. Without thinking, I felt as my hands released a surge of power and found my power gripping at Byrein's shoulder, trying to stop it.

"Stop this!" I screeched into his mind.

He shoved me out and ripped his shoulder from my power's grip. I heard as he released a hot breath from his flared nostrils. His wings flung out, blocking my view from the boy. All I could do was watch Winona as she fought to break free from the man who held her back. She screamed for her son. But all I heard was my heart inside my ears and my breath release.

The boy's lifeless body crumpled to the ground.

"Take her away for her treason," Byrein commanded.

A hush drew across the crowd. I watched as they dragged Winona away kicking and screaming. She lurched over and over for her son, until she was out of sight. The man once holding Velkin back slung the boy's limp body over a shoulder, just behind Byrein's outstretched wings, and walked away, leaving the crowd of onlookers dazed.

Byrein didn't turn. He didn't tuck his wings away. He stood with hands crumpled in fists, still riffled with frustration. I managed to lift my head and look at the faces around me.

Their eyes were on me, not Byrein. They looked to me for guidance. They looked to me for security.

Byrein had taken one of their own. Their neighbor. Their friend.

And if I wasn't mistaken, they knew I tried to stop him.

fourteen

Byrein made it clear that I was to join him and the others for dinner that evening, after I had gathered myself. He insisted on meeting me at my tent, which felt like the setup for a trap.

I knew that I had defied him that afternoon. I was expected to support his decisions and he was quiet toward me all afternoon, making it feel like I was flying through a thornbush. One wrong move and I would get stuck.

He didn't speak to me after the encounter with Winona and Velkin. He didn't even so much as look in my direction. He gave me the silent treatment and allowed me the pleasure of waiting in antagonizing anticipation for his reprimanding over my actions.

I was so exhausted from the afternoon that when Byrein returned me to my tent, I collapsed into the bed. I don't remember sleeping, exactly, just resting and allowing my brain to run amuck. It was the kind of exhaustion that hits you when you are overwhelmed and your mind won't stop, but your body feels like gelatin.

When I finally decided to get myself back up, I was groggy and unrested. I had hoped to feel rejuvenated, but my body had other plans. I slipped my feet into shoes and sat at the edge of my bed. For a moment, I sat, listening and waiting. I searched the space for Byrein's presence.

I was completely alone. No sign of him spying on me. Likely too furious to do so right now. Carefully, I lifted the sheet back and stared at the notches I had placed for my time here. I didn't bother counting them. I knew I was behind at least five.

With my foot, I hooked the strap of a

messenger-style bag that sat underneath my bed and slid it into the candlelit space. I lifted it carefully and dusted it off, to fold back the top flap. Thumbing through, I looked at the supplies Renae had helped me collect. Two changes of clothes. A couple of fire starters. A canteen for water. A few extra hair-ties. And a long coat.

Taking a mental note for my own reassurance, I folded the flap over the bag and tucked it safely out of sight under my bed again. I adjusted the sheet overhanging on the bed once more to hide away its secrets, just as Millie entered the tent.

She stood at the opening and didn't take a step closer. She didn't look at me. She didn't move. It was unusual behavior for her.

"You are summoned for dinner," she stated, keeping her eyes low.

"Okay," I remarked.

She wrung her fingers and looked jittery. Uncomfortable. She opened her mouth and closed it again, trying to decide if she would speak the words dancing so closely to her teeth. Finally, her eyes darted up and then around the tent. She glanced a look behind her.

"I'm not supposed to talk to you," she

whispered hastily. "I have direct orders not to. From Byrein himself. But there is talk through the Encampment. We know you tried to stop Byrein. We know you tried to save one of our own from him. Everyone is confused right now. About Velkin being powerless, about Byrein's display—"

I nodded softly. I didn't know what to say. I didn't know how to comfort her. She witnessed a tragedy today. It was clear she didn't know how to process.

Some footsteps walked past the tent, followed by conversation.

"That woman got what she deserved. She brought a powerless one into our home," spoke a raspy voice.

I clenched my jaw.

"Do you think she really didn't know? I mean she kept screaming how the father was like us," another deeper voice commented.

"No way. She was just hoping we wouldn't find out. The woman is a lunatic, bringin' her spawn into our home like that. And Byrein took care of that for us. Just like he always does. Those powerless winged creatures don't deserve to exist in this world. One less of those wasteful disgraces in the world, I say."

Millie had backed up to the opening once more. Her thoughts seemed conflicted. She seemed to think that the man was maybe right. She didn't believe that powerless creatures should exist, but on the other hand, we had spent time with this one. Spent time with Winona. They were people Byrein convinced would be safe here.

Millie shook her head. She took one last glance at me and returned her eyes to the ground and exited the tent. I watched for a moment as the tent flap swayed and settled once more. A leaf made its way inside from the breezy outside world. It rolled along its curled spine, tumbling away from the wind, until halting to a stop against the tassel of the rug by my feet.

I gathered myself and stood. My feet found stability and so did my wings. My frustrations were swarming my mind and my anxieties were riddled through my body. I knew I was expected. I knew I had to go. I knew I had no choice. I wanted to run. I wanted this to be my escape. But I knew I wouldn't get far. Byrein's guards were likely going to be waiting for me.

Just a little longer, Es. You've survived this long. I

took a sigh and shook the uncertainties from my shoulders. I wanted to yell and scream and be angry. I needed to, but I knew I couldn't.

I struck a spark to my finger and played with it to ease my veins. With a snap, I snuffed it back out and watched a spark drift to the ground and lick the dry, curled leaf at the corner of the rug below me. A puff of smoke occurred, and I watched the leaf catch fire. For a moment, I let it burn before stamping it out with the bottom of my shoe and exiting my designated tent.

A golden glow graced the pathway, as the sun began to set for another fall evening. The air was crisp and cool, sending a shiver through my spine. I watched above as a few clouds were moving in from the horizon. I could hear a couple of Byrein's guards trailing far behind me, likely to keep an eye on my position after my little stunt with Byrein. I didn't pay them any attention.

I passed a new clearing and watched as a woman dressed in all black waved a hand. She stood firm and kept her knees bent to brace herself for the task she was given. A new canvas-sided tent slid up from the ground and set itself perfectly into the dirt below as if it were a puppet being controlled by a puppeteer.

Byrein was waiting just outside of the dining tent when I arrived. His eyes caught my face, and I tried my best to keep my usual face of stone even more blank this evening. I didn't want to give him the satisfaction of knowing he terrified me. He raised an eyebrow and I joined him at his side, feeling a little smaller than usual.

A new face greeted him with a proud bow and passed me by as if I were just another object to walk around. Byrein peered down at me, his scar along his jaw more distinct in the shadows of the evening. He looked tired in his vile, dark eyes, and I couldn't help but find snarky enjoyment in that. I watched and waited for him to direct us inside.

Part of me expected him to finally get around to reprimanding me. Finally yell in my face. To snap at my actions that occurred earlier that evening. He just glared past me. He wanted me aware that he was angry but waited and held his tongue.

I think I would have rather been yelled at. This waiting was worse.

Moments later, he pulled the opening back for the tent and waved me inside. His face changed from stern and disappointed to happy and charismatic.

His subjects commented words of praise for putting that woman in her place, as they called it. They reminisced how it was feeling more and more like the place that Destimov had created. It all seemed fake. Like it was scripted. Like they were saying what they should to keep on his good side and make him chipper.

Some were telling the truth. They agreed with today's events. Some were lying straight through their teeth. It was obvious for those that they were just hoping not to be next on Byrein's bad side.

A couple individuals commented to me that I was "lucky" to follow in his footsteps. I wasn't sure what it was they intended about that. But whatever it was, I didn't like the feeling it gave me in my gut. The feeling that I was being associated with Byrein. And that I was being compared to him.

Dinner was long and monotonous. Much of the same conversations. Byrein, however, was really laying it on thick. He would have a comment and then glance at me to make sure I had caught his backhanded remark. He never directly stated anything to me, but made the others think that he was just "so very happy" to have me, his queen, by his side.

"My Queen, my Esmari, makes me certain of my decisions. It's *wonderful* to know that she supports the cause," he said to Renae.

Renae didn't dare look in my direction. She was too starry-eyed gazing at Byrein, who sought out to speak to her for something other than a command he expected her to fulfill. She tried not to cringe at his pet names for me.

Byrein didn't seem to notice her. He enjoyed the attention and enjoyed bragging of his accomplishments. Most of all, I think he knew just how uncomfortable he was making me.

"Smile," he demanded. It was the first word he spoke directly to me since this afternoon.

I fought the urge to roll my eyes at him. I didn't smile, but for fear of his wrath, I did soften my stone face, just a little.

The room slowly cleared out after everyone had eaten. A few people from the meeting this morning nodded to me and thanked me for my contributions to the cause. It disgusted me. I didn't offer words in return, just a nod or a look to acknowledge their presence, to keep them and Byrein at bay.

Byrein finished his conversation with a woman

I had seen a few other times. She had a pitchy voice and always had on a sour face. Like she just licked a lemon. She never laughed or smiled, but I liked to think that if she did laugh, it would sound like an annoying squeaky toy that children played with.

I was hoping to find a time to excuse myself back to my tent for the night. To somehow get away from the awkward conversation I didn't want to be a part of. And most of all be away from Byrein and his punishment of silence.

"I think that it is time I took my Esmari for an evening stroll," Byrein concluded to the woman. She nodded and left without another word.

fifteen

Byrein motioned for me to follow him from the tent. He didn't seem upset or angry. But he also was decided in his motion. He knew I would follow. He knew I would obey his silent command.

A guard opened the tent flap for us and nodded his head as we walked through. I pulled at the body of the shirt I wore, realizing just how wrinkled and dusty it looked. I didn't even bother to change my clothes for dinner. Honestly, who was I meaning to impress anyway?

We wandered down a path which grew increasingly quieter. The cold of the night had everyone tucked away inside their tents, leaving the outside world barren and vulnerable. Even the guards, Byrein's right hand men, were excused for the evening.

We made our way to seclusion, and I waited. I listened for Byrein to tear into me. Anticipated what his words were going to be. Waited to see if he would even talk or just take me out altogether. *This is it. Byrein isn't going to let me live to see another day. You took it too far this time, Es.*

Suddenly, Byrein stopped. He spun on his heel. The charismatic leader was no longer present. That calm and chatty man was left inside the dining tent. Instead, there was rage and wrath burning in his eyes. He stared me down. Closer and closer he stepped. His hair shone in the moonlight, just a piece out of place. He didn't bother fixing it. His clean-shaven face was stern and determined.

"I chose you," he sneered through his teeth, enunciating each word. "I saw potential in you. You are to be my successor. My partner. Someday, my *wife*. I gave you a home! I showed you your potential.

I gave you followers that will one day be yours. Followers for you to rule over. I showed you just how cruel this world can be and how we are responsible for cleansing it!"

I tried to stand firm. I stared him down. I tried not to waver. *Hold your tongue. Show no fear.* My heart felt like it was going to pound right out of my chest. Carefully, I took a breath.

He huffed. Gawked even. Flinging out his wings, he made himself as large and menacing as he could. He darted close to me and glared right in my eyes. Thankfully, I didn't flinch. I glared directly back.

"You defied me! You, of all people, Esmari!" Byrein hissed. It was the first time he had called me by just my name here. "You have no right! You will *never* defy me again. Do you hear me? You are destined to take over my reign. I hand-picked you for that and so much greatness that goes with! Once you hold my power, you will rule all of what I have left for you. It's what I have been preparing you for!"

"I never wanted any of this, you delusional monster!" I thundered.

He circled me, stopping at my back. I glanced over my shoulder at him and watched as he brought up two fingers. He didn't try to be gentle, or secretive. My heart dropped as he jabbed his fingers just below my shoulder blade.

I could feel my power acting weird inside of my body. Like my power was getting sleepy, tingling all through my veins.

"I made you…" Byrein sneered. "And if you aren't careful, I can destroy you. Don't forget, I'm a Mind Sight, too. I can relieve you of your power if you try a stunt like that ever again."

I stopped thinking and allowed my power and my body to take over. My fight, flight, or freeze mode was kicking in, and for once it chose fight.

My body turned and I had his wrist in my hand before he could even think twice. I allowed my power to seep from my hands and my wings to fill out at my back.

I thought of fire.

The reds and oranges of a threatening flame. I wanted him to burn. I wanted him to know the extent of my power. To know my overwhelming terror. I watched as the power engulfed my arms and pressed into his wrist. The sizzle of my power against his skin was plenty for him to understand.

He let out a gasp and ripped his arm from my

clutch, my handprint still branded on his wrist. I stepped back and allowed my power to grow. I didn't want to hold back. I wanted him to see my strength. I allowed my hands to meet one another and watched as the red smoke surrounded me and, in turn, him.

His pupils dilated. I knew he was both impressed and infuriated by my display. He gripped at his arm, likely in pain, and clenched his jaw. I didn't care. Nothing else mattered except making sure he knew just who he was messing with.

"Do you forget just what *your Esmari* is?" I raged. "You may be a Mind Sight, but you will never be a True Sage."

I glared him down, threatening his very existence. I was shaking with fear inside, but on the outside, I tried my best to put on the most menacing display possible. He didn't back down. If anything, I could tell he was growing angrier at my encounter. Furious that I didn't follow him like all the others. Seething that I dared to have an opinion and a thought of my own which didn't align with his. And most of all raging that I didn't fear him.

"Mark my words, you are nothing without me. I will make sure of it," Byrein warned.

He flashed one more glare as I allowed my power to fade out of my hands and arms. There was a smirk behind his eyes. He convinced himself with those last words directed at me that he had won. Confidently, he turned and walked away, leaving me completely alone.

sixteen

I waited for a moment, allowing the initial shock of the encounter to wear off and listening until Byrein's footsteps were no longer heard. And then it hit me. No one knew where I was. Only Byrein. No one was watching me. No one was accompanying me. It was just me and the moon.

In Byrein's egotistical confidence that made him think he won the argument, he forgot one key element. Me. He walked me out here. On his own.

And he was likely under the impression that I was too afraid of him to test him any further.

He could have hurt me. And I could have hurt him. He knew just to what extent that I could have. Did he think that he struck fear into me? That I lacked the confidence to be anything without him?

I mulled over the words he said for another moment. He made it clear that he could take my power, so does that mean I could take his?

No, Es. No time to think about that. A whistle of wind through the trees shook me to my senses. I touched my necklace, which somehow remained with me through all of this. The small black onyx stone sat next to a now-chipped jade one. I twisted at the chain, thinking through my next actions carefully.

You need to escape.

I spread my wings and flicked into the air, darting as fast as I could fly to my tent, thankful for my wings to be as black as the shadows of the night. My mind raced, knowing that this all had to go just right.

I watched for any sign of movement. Any indication that I was being watched. Watched by Byrein. Watched by his inner circle. By his guards.

But the crisp air and preparations for Phase Two made the Encampment seem deserted.

I was grateful to feel completely and utterly alone for once. It was a feeling I had embraced because I had to, being here for so long. Only a select few were allowed to be my company, and Byrein was the top of that list.

But none of them were company I wanted to keep. All were twisted killers. All were sick-minded individuals with horrid morals. All of them followed a leader who turned his back on his own following.

My tent felt off when I landed just next to the opening. I could tell there was a spooky energy about the space, and when I entered, I knew just why that was.

My tent was a complete mess. Anything and everything in the space had been riffled through. The dresses in the wardrobe were torn in shreds. And I am not going to lie, the sight made me almost smile. But when I saw the messenger bag strap hanging off my bed, my heart sank.

It sat empty. The canteen for water was missing a lid. I only could find one set of clothing. A pair of pants sat on the side with a tear at the knee. The shirt seam was torn at two places. And the sock was missing its pair. It was as if someone rampaged through my tent.

I felt a presence behind me and turned to face it head on.

"I can't let you leave," Renae whispered.

"You did this?" I asked, confused. "But I thought you wanted me gone?"

"I want Byrein happy. And I realized today that if you aren't here, he won't ever be happy. I'd rather him be satisfied, even if it means you are by his side," Renae responded. There was sorrow and pain in her words, but I could tell she had made up her mind.

"I need to go, you don't understand," I spoke softly.

"I do understand. I understand that you are running from the home Byrein has created for you. Ever since he first discovered you, he has done *everything* for you. To prepare this whole place for you. And I am not going to let you walk away from all of it. I'm not going to let you tear him down," she pleaded.

Her hand raised and her eyes grew still. She was attempting to use her power on me. Except in her delusional rampage of trying to stop me, she forgot that she has no power over a Mind Sight like me.

I did the only thing I could think to do. I rushed to face her back and pressed two fingers firmly below her shoulder blade. I found the source of her power and pinched, just hard enough to temporarily paralyze it. Something I admittedly learned from Byrein.

I knew it wouldn't be enough. I needed her not to follow me. Not to sound the alarm. Someone was bound to see her head this way. Maybe they would think she was here to stand guard over me, like she had so many times before.

"I'm sorry," I whispered.

I flicked a spark of power to my finger and allowed the electric Energy to find her essence. I watched her jolt as I pressed it against her, just long enough to daze her, leaving a small burn mark against her neck.

Carefully, I lowered her down to the ground. She stared and mumbled something, but I didn't catch what it was, nor did I have time to.

Quickly, I shoved what I could find into the messenger bag, not attempting to make it neat or tidy. I found a hair-tie and yanked it onto my wrist. A sigh of relief left my lips as I saw the arm of the long black coat peeking out from behind the chair in the corner. I shrugged it on and tossed the messenger bag back across my body.

I took one more look around the tent and felt joy in leaving it behind. The late nights. The notches on the bedframe. The lost time. The scratchy fabric of the dresses ripped to shreds, scattered across the floor. The dusty rug.

I hoped to see none of them ever again.

seventeen

Silently, I exited my tent. I moved with the shadows. Ducking at any given sound. I kept my senses on high alert for Byrein's presence to be watching me. My power tingled inside my arms, feeling all the energy and tension from the outside world. My Mind Sight stayed at bay, which I found myself to be grateful for. I didn't need the distraction right now.

I wanted to fly, but I feared that with the

brightness of the moon, I may cast a shadow too easy to detect. Plus, flying meant more sound. More wind created. More possibilities to be seen. And a whole lot less places to hide.

Move quickly. Don't stop for too long. Don't leave a trace.

I hadn't realized just how large the Encampment was. How spread out the territory really was. Tent after tent. Tree after tree. It felt like it would go on forever.

I scurried to the back side of the next tent and waited as I heard footsteps pass by. I held my breath, watching them approach my tent. *Please don't go in. Please don't go in.*

They continued without a pause, and I released a tense breath. Tucking a stray strand of my tangled sandy blonde hair behind my ear, I continued to the next shadow.

I slipped behind a crate. Then another tent. A clearing appeared and I darted swiftly for the large tree at the far end.

CRUNCH.

My foot met a pile of leaves and I frantically looked around to see if anyone heard. A man peeked out from the flap of his tent, and I glued myself to the trunk of the tree, tucking every last inch of me into its shadow. The man's eyes glinted from the moonlight, and he peered right in my direction. I held my breath. A quiet voice called him back inside. With a shrug he rejoined them.

I retraced the map I had seen in my mind. I was focused and determined to see the edge of the Encampment that was closest to Banshui. From there, it was an almost direct line to the outskirts of the West District. I held the image in my brain. Hoping that I had read it correctly. Hoping I was heading in the right direction.

I darted from tree to tree, careful of my step. I slinked over roots and dodged the satisfyingly crunchy leaves. I flittered momentarily to fling myself from one shadow into another. My heart raced. I could feel my breath become heavier. I knew I had to be getting closer.

Another clearing, and little to no shadow from trees. Just a single tent, set aside from the others. One I hadn't seen before. Maybe I hadn't ventured into this part of the Encampment in all my time here. Maybe I just never paid attention.

I stayed where I was hidden, trying my best to devise a plan while observing my surroundings. I could see my destination just up ahead. My freedom was moments away, but I needed to safely get there. I looked once more at the tent in my path.

The flaps were tied back, and I watched as the candlelight flickered inside, revealing two individuals. One paced the tent, their wings and arms tucked behind their back. They were indecisive and didn't say a word. As if they didn't have any more in them. The other sat against a post with their arms tethered to it, above their head.

I looked closer and realized just who it was.

Winona.

My breath caught in my throat as I looked over her. From what I could see, her hair was a mess, and she had a scratch stretching across her face. Her shirt was torn, and she panted, trying to catch air in her lungs.

I waited for the man pacing to turn his back, hoping Winona wouldn't catch sight of me either. *Three. Two. One. Now!*

I ran as swiftly and quietly as my legs would take me. Flicking a look back, I saw the man begin to turn his head, and then his body. I flicked my wings to push myself the rest of the way into the shadow of the overhanging branches and slid to the base of the tree to catch my breath.

I was in the final stretch. I was going to survive. I was going to escape this prison.

Prison.

The word resonated in my mind and brought back the image of Winona sitting inside the tent. Tethered. Bloody. Hurting. Alone.

Oh flitters, Esmari.

I turned back toward the tent and watched as the man inside paced once more. He paused midway through and said something to Winona, wagging his finger at her. I tried to understand what it was that he was saying.

Suddenly, he turned and began walking out of the tent. I ducked behind the tree trunk and sandwiched the messenger bag to my side, to prevent it from swaying. I took another peek out and watched the man walk away with haste.

I knew there wasn't much time. *Now's your chance.*

I listened to a gust of wind begin in the tree's leaves. With a flap, my wings matching the sound of the wind, I flung myself to the tent's opening. I crept inside, staying low to the ground in case there was another inside I didn't account for. When I found the coast to be clear, I rushed to Winona.

Her eyes met mine and welled up with tears from the sight of a familiar face. I placed a finger to my mouth to warn her to keep quiet. I wasn't sure just how far the man wandered, and I wasn't about to find out.

I pulled at the tethers, trying to free her. She pulled too, but shook her head in disappointment.

"It's no use," she whispered.

I looked around frantically for anything sharp to use. Anything to cut her free. But the tent was stripped from anything remotely useful. *Think, Es. Think!*

"Go, before he comes back," she cooed. She had all but accepted her fate.

With a gasp, I looked at my hand. I flicked a spark to my fingertip and flung it right at the fraying part of the cord tethering her wrists. I watched as it ate right through and snuffed out on the wooden post. Together we pulled, and the cord gave way with a snap.

Relieved, I smiled at her and helped her up.

"How do you feel about escaping this horrible place?" I smirked with a whisper.

She nodded, and I watched a tear roll down her

cheek.

She paused. "But won't they try to look for me?"

I thought for a moment. She was right. I was prepared to be hunted down by Byrein. She didn't deserve that. She already lost her son today and was tortured and interrogated. She was accused by the leader himself of treason. She would be hunted down.

I looked at my hands once more and thought of the flames. I thought of the destruction I could cause. I thought of the face Byrein would have in seeing it. Byrein would be to blame for not one, but two lives from the community. Not a soul would know what destruction I was capable of. No one except Byrein. And that sweet taste of revenge sounded just too good to pass up.

"Tear off that strand hanging from your shirt. They won't know what hit them," I remarked. "There's no way you could have survived."

I flicked a look to Winona, who returned the look with worry. Carefully taking the fabric from her, I placed a Sage Energy engulfed hand against it and watched it smolder into a flame. I tossed it at the corner of the tent, allowing it to touch the canvas sides. A mist was rolling in and I sent sparks of my power into it, listening as it zapped and danced along the droplets. I didn't control it. I set it free. I let it run. I watched it cause destruction.

Winona glanced at me and watched as the flame was settling. She flung her hands up and brought a gust of air to fuel the fire. We both watched as it grew into a warm, bright escape.

I pulled at Winona's arm to get her to leave and observed as she raced on ahead of me, ducking into what shadow she could find, now fighting the firelight and the moon. I followed after her, pausing once more to admire my work.

Flinging both hands out, I allowed my hands and arms to emit power stronger than I had ever done before. I pressed my palms together and formed a large crimson ball of swirling Energy. With one last breath, I launched it at the top of the tent and watched it come crushing down, leaving the tent in a heap of smoldering red smoke.

That was just for you, Byrein.

I saw someone dart up into the sky in the distance and heard footsteps nearby racing toward the fire. I snapped back into reality. Grabbing at Winona's elbow once more, I yanked at her to run.

No regard for the shadows. No regard for

hiding. There shouldn't be anything more on this side of the Encampment. No more Exes to run into. No more tents. Just trees and freedom.

We ran faster and faster. We panted and kept going. I kept an eye on where I knew the edge of Byrein's territory would be. The edge of the Encampment. The edge of this prison.

I ran for it, jumping over stumps and exposed tree roots. Dodging tree branches. Fluttering only when necessary. I could hear Winona panting beside me. Her feet hitting each step on the ground with a thud.

A sob left her lips as she gasped for air. I didn't even realize she had been crying. It made sense. After all that had happened today. After her leader betrayed her. After her son was killed before her eyes.

I may not agree with her views, but I knew deep down those views changed today. I knew she was different from the others. I knew that if she could, she would have saved her son and lived a peaceful life with him.

She saw first-hand the malice of Byrein. And it was her son who helped to show it to the Encampment as a whole. Byrein divided his people in one act. And that is something that just might come back and bite him.

As we drew closer and closer to the edge of the Encampment, a wave washed over me. A wave of excitement and anxiety. A wave of peace and overwhelm.

I knew that I was going to be free of this place. Free from wearing something a man tells me to wear. Free from performing "experiments" on volunteers. Free from the mental torture and exhaustion. Free from being someone I was not, just to survive another day.

I couldn't explain the excitement that was bubbling up inside of me. The disbelief that I was living to see the day I escaped this place. The pure joy in the idea of not spending every day with the horrible leader of the Exes.

I wouldn't have to watch what I said and how I held my face. I wouldn't have keep myself from reacting to someone. I wouldn't have to watch someone's every move and guess if they were happy or mad. Or guess if they were going to flip a switch and lose their temper.

I wouldn't have to take in power unwillingly just to keep a man at bay. Nor did I have to learn his ways of leading a community I didn't want to be a part of. Let alone, how to cleanse the world one region at a time. I wouldn't have to contribute to the terror. To entertain the discussion of the powerless and their place in this world.

No more.

I could finally be myself. I could breathe and smile. I could discover who I was again and who I wanted to be. Not who someone else told me to be. I could talk about something other than my next experiment I was expected to perform.

The trees broke way for a clearing and a grassy hill. Down below, a new forest began, filled with new trees and new security. I thought back to the map and took note of what direction to take for the next leg of my journey.

For a moment, Winona and I paused. I looked out over the horizon, listening as the commotion of the fire she and I caused began to fade from our ears. The wind played with fallen leaves down in the grassy valley before us. Winona smiled and I sighed. We made it.

I was free.

And the first place I wanted to go was home to Banshui.

Home is known for having a meaning of serenity. It's where you can be yourself without the worry or disappointing anyone. It is supposed to restore you and calm you.

I didn't know just how much that meant to me. How important having a place to truly call your home meant. That is, until it was stripped from existence in my life. The word was abused and overused as if Byrein were trying to convince me. And it worked for a time. It confused me. I was unsure where I belonged.

But now, as I look over the valley before me, I have a destination in mind when I think of home. And that, in itself, is the most comforting feeling in the world.